IN THE
VALLEY
OF THE
SHADOW

IN THE
VALLEY
OF THE
SHADOW

J.R. MARTIN

TATE PUBLISHING
AND ENTERPRISES, LLC

Published by Tate Publishing & Enterprises, LLC
127 E. Trade Center Terrace | Mustang, Oklahoma 73064 USA
1.888.361.9473 | www.tatepublishing.com

Tate Publishing is committed to excellence in the publishing industry. The company reflects the philosophy established by the founders, based on Psalm 68:11,
"The Lord gave the word and great was the company of those who published it."

Book design copyright © 2014 by Tate Publishing, LLC. All rights reserved.
Cover design by Jim Villaflores
Interior design by Joana Quilantang

Published in the United States of America

ISBN: 978-1-63418-393-2
Biography & Autobiography / Personal Memoirs
14.09.24

To those struggling to overcome addictions that have taken them where they didn't want to go, and kept them far longer than they wanted to stay

Acknowledgment

The book *In the Valley of the Shadow* is a biography of an amazing woman. It has been my pleasure and privilege to get to know her well. We have worked side by side for many hours and shared our stories and our heartaches. Through this time together, I have come to know her deep and abiding love for Jesus Christ. I have come to know her disappointment and her heartache, but also her joys and laughter and all that Christ has done for her.

Shelia Carter, I love you and appreciate you. I hope this book brings you many rewards and perhaps closures to some of the things you have endured. I thank you for your candid words and actions. I pray for you daily and want you to know I shall always count you as one of my dearest and sweetest friends.

To those of you who are still wondering if God is real, I assure you he is. Only he could have saved this vivacious young woman. Only he could have reached into the pits of hell and removed her from its clutches. Only he can continue to bless her and her loved ones with an undeniable love. Only he is the same yesterday, today, and forever. God bless you as you read.

Names have been changed to protect the innocent.

INTRODUCTION

Inside the pages of this book, you will find inspiration and hope for a better tomorrow. You will walk hand in hand with a dope addict, an alcoholic, sexual promiscuity, and death. You will wail in the chambers of Satan's lyre as he seeks to destroy Anne Marie and her entire family.

You have a front row seat to a life so scarred that only Jesus could repair it. You will walk with Anne Marie through the valley of the shadow and rejoice with her as she finally stands in the sunlight with the shadows falling behind her. You will wonder how she survived intact and filled with hope for a brighter tomorrow.

Find a comfortable seat, put on your reading glasses, if required, and prepare to be filled with shock and wonder. It is the hope of the author and the person whom the book is about, that you will see Jesus at work, firsthand. The book reads like fiction, but rest assured, it's all true. From a little five-year-old child to a grown woman facing an ex-Marine counselor, you will see the very soul of a woman as it is laid bare before you.

The names in the book are fictitious in order to protect the innocent, but each character named lived, breathed, and played an important role in the life of Anne Marie. When you finish reading the book, it is the hope of the author you will say, "There but for the grace of God, go I."

1

Anne Marie heard the unmistaken shuffle of his muddy boots coming down the hall, and she knew what would happen next. She tried to crawl under the covers and hide her small body. She prayed he would think she was asleep and go away. He entered her room and walked to her bedside, she held her breath trying not to breathe, but she could not hold back a gasp as he threw back the covers. Her small five-year-old body clad in her little girl pink nightgown shook under his huge hand. His labored breathing and whiskey breath made her want to throw up, but she dared not call for Momma. He had told her he would kill all of them if she told.

This one act of violation set the scene for the next twenty-five years of Anne Marie's life. A life filled with drugs, alcohol, perversion, and low self-esteem followed her like a relentless bloodhound trying to snatch her life away just as he had snatched away her childhood innocence. As an adult, the nightmares tore at her mind just as he had torn at her clothes. She would awake screaming and begging him to leave her alone. But she knew he never would, just like he never did when she was a small child. She called him Johnny, and he was her daddy.

The road was rough, and the pickup bounced along what felt like a rub board. Momma was driving, and Johnny and Anne Marie were riding in the back. Anne Marie's sisters, Rachel and Maddie, and her little brother, Cade, were in the cab with Momma. Momma had to drive because Johnny was too drunk. They were on their way to Granny and Poppa's. Granny and Poppa were Momma's parents. Their house was the only place Anne Marie ever felt safe. Johnny leaned over and whispered, "You gonna give me some tonight, little girl, you can count on it."

Something inside of Anne Marie snapped, and she started hitting the back window of the pickup. She was fourteen, and all of a sudden, she didn't care what happened to her or anyone else. She just knew Johnny was never touching her again. Momma slowed down, and Anne Marie jumped out of the truck. She started running down the road. Momma accelerated the old truck and soon caught up with her. "Get in this truck right now," she told Anne Marie.

Anne Marie just kept running. She ignored Momma and Johnny ordering her to get back in the truck. She didn't care what Momma or Johnny said to her. Soon Granny and Poppa's house came into view. She slowed her run to a walk and watched as Momma and Johnny sped by her to reach the house before she did. The speeding truck kicked up dust from the gravel road and caused her to cough, but she just kept walking. She watched as Momma and Johnny and her siblings exited the pickup in front of Granny's house. She knew they would tell her grandparents that she was just mad and spoiled, but she didn't care. She had had enough. She didn't care about the lies told on her anymore, and she had made up her mind that the beatings and molestation from Johnny were over.

She reached Granny and Poppa's old farm house and had to stop at the gate to catch her breath. Her eyes were swollen from crying and her face dirty from the dusty road. Snot and tears mingled on her face, and her heart raced in her chest. But she was ready to do what she had to do.

She stepped on the porch, and the weathered boards creaked beneath her feet. Granny and Poppa saw her, and the look on their faces told her they were concerned. Momma's brother, Uncle Jim, also had a look of confusion. Anne Marie took a deep breath, and then she said, "Granny, my daddy has been abusing me for years. It started when I was five years old. Now he's started in on Rachel. I don't know the proper word for it, but I know it's wrong. Daddies are supposed to protect their children, not make them do things that are bad. He told me if I told you, he would kill Momma and all of you and us. But I can't take anymore. He has got to stop."

Poppa got up and left the room in the middle of Johnny's denial. When he reentered, he had his shotgun. He pointed it straight at Johnny and said, "Get out of my house now. Don't ever come back. Get out of my house in town that you are living in. You are a monster that doesn't deserve to draw another breath, and if you ever even try to touch any of my granddaughters again, I will blow you to hell, do you understand?"

Johnny nodded his head. He wasn't so drunk that he couldn't understand what Poppa told him. Anne Marie watched as he stepped off the porch and started walking back toward town. He didn't look so mean anymore. He just looked like a weak man slowly walking out of her life. Anne Marie thanked God, and for the first time, she realized it was God who had given her the courage to finally tell the truth about Johnny. The next day, Granny went with her to the police department to press charges on the man who had scarred her life forever.

2

After the day Anne Marie found the courage to expose Johnny, life was good. Momma actually smiled, and all the kids laughed a lot. They now lived with Granny and Poppa, and at night, she could lie down on a good soft bed and close her eyes with no fear.

Johnny had to stay away from them, but he could still call Momma, and call he did. There's no doubt that Momma was as sick as Johnny, but in a different way. Momma had been beaten, raped, kicked, and intimidated until she was so downtrodden she couldn't defend her children or herself. But she held out as long as she could.

Summer rolled around, and school was out. Everyday Granny paid for the kids to go swimming at the city swimming pool. Anne Marie's job as the oldest was to watch Rachel, Maddie, and two-year-old Cade. She didn't mind. She had been doing that for years. So with one eye on Cade, she would stretch out on the pool side and work on her tan. One day, this really cute guy spoke to her. Her heart skipped a beat. He had beautiful long brown hair and the most beautiful eyes she had ever looked into. He was great on the diving board and would splash her every time he got the chance. He was Anne Marie's first real boyfriend. He would give them rides home in his Pappy's old car. She invited him in one day to meet her Momma. His name was Cliff Moore, and he was gorgeous to her. They started spending a lot of time together, watching movies, and going to the swimming pool. He even taught her little brother, Cade, to swim and not be afraid of the water. He would take Anne Marie to a drive in and buy her root beer floats. This was the closest she had ever been to real dating. She was in love. They would slip off to the woods and have sex. It was nothing like it had been with Johnny. She didn't feel dirty.

One day, Annie Marie told him about Johnny and what he had done to her. She was afraid he might not like her anymore after that, but she wanted him to know. That night, he told her that he went home and cried for her. He even beat his guitar against a tree out of anguish over what had happened to her. He then came back, and he still wanted to see her. No one had ever cried for her before and felt the pain that she had felt. After that, they started talking about getting married. They were fifteen and sixteen at the time. She dreamed of spending their lives together. She wanted to grow old with him and be like her Granny and Poppa and have the kind of relationship they had over many years.

Cliff lived with his grandparents who raised him. The first time Anne Marie met them, his grand-pappy was in his boxers out in the back yard, taking a shower with the water hose. "Pappy," as Cliff called him, was a large man. He made Granny look small beside him. They were both alcoholics, but Anne Marie didn't mind because they were nothing like the alcoholic she knew. Pappy would drink Jim Bean Whiskey, and Granny drank vodka. They weren't violent or mean. They were usually just funny. Granny used to have a band, and she was the lead singer. The band would play on the radio, and she would sing and dance. That's where Cliff got his musical talent. Cliff could play the guitar really well, and he also had a band. They played heavy metal, and Cliff loved the band Kiss.

During this time, Johnny had been calling Momma day and night. He promised if she would just forgive him, he would stop drinking and go to counseling and do whatever she asked him to do. When Momma told Anne Marie she was going back to Johnny, Anne Marie couldn't believe her ears. "You're actually going back to that lowlife after you know what he did to me? He won't stop drinking or abusing, Momma! Have you lost your mind?" But Momma wouldn't listen, and she went back to him.

Anne Marie told her Momma that she and Cliff were getting married. Momma tried to talk her out of it, and Anne Marie let her know she was never going home again. Whether Momma would sign for her and Cliff to marry or not, she was through with Johnny and the home life she had. If she didn't sign, then they would just move in together anyway.

When Momma told Johnny what Anne Marie had said, he cautiously approached Cliff and her. He told them if she would move back home to make Momma happy, they could live in the backroom of the house, and they would sign for her to get married.

Cliff and Anne Marie were young, and all they could think about was getting married and being together all the time. Cliff's grandparents had agreed to sign for him when he told them all the things Anne Marie had endured when she lived at home. So they all signed, and Anne Marie and Cliff started making wedding plans.

3

Family and friends united to help make Anne Marie and Cliff's wedding one that would make memories for years to come. Anne Marie's Uncle Ted was dating a girl who had the most beautiful wedding dress Anne Marie had ever seen. The woman's parents had spent over $2,000.00 on the dress, and since the woman was getting a divorce, she wanted to get rid of the dress. Anne Marie felt like Cinderella as she tried on the dress, and Granny pined and tucked to make it fit her just right.

The day of the wedding, Anne Marie was so nervous she thought her heart would leap right out of her chest. She busied herself by doing her hair and nails and packing her an overnight bag. All she could think about was Cliff. He was going to be her husband, and she was going to make him the best wife any man could ever want.

Anne Marie stood outside the church as the organist started playing the wedding march. She carefully climbed the three steps leading to the front church doors and stood looking inside with a look of awe. She had never seen a more beautiful church all filled with flowers and people. Standing at the front of the church's altar was Cliff, and her heart just melted when she saw him. He looked so handsome standing there with all his groomsmen and the preacher. Anne Marie hesitated for a moment when she saw Johnny. She hated him so much that just looking at him made her anger rise until she could feel the burning in her throat. She quickly put her gaze on Cliff and walked down the aisle to become his wife.

The wedding reception was so wonderful until her cousins dragged her outside and pushed her in the car. They planned to go to the local radio station and announce live where Cliff could find his new bride. When they got there, the radio announcer said there was a ball game on, and he couldn't interrupt to make their announcement. So they started back to the church. When they got there, they found a disgruntled groom who was so upset at what they had done. He was cussing and throwing his arms up. Quickly, the cousins departed the church grounds, leaving Cliff and Anne Marie alone. Anne Marie tore her dress as she climbed in the borrowed car Cliff had acquired for the night. She looked at Cliff and slid across the seat to be next to him. Like kids, they drove through Jack in the Box to get something to eat and let all their friends see their car, covered in shaving cream and declaring "Just Married," in bold soapy letters. But soon they were at the motel where Cliff had rented the bridal suite for the night with some money given to them as wedding present.

Anne Marie woke the next morning with a feeling of relief. She had slept close to Cliff all night, and his arms around her made her feel that she was the safest person in the whole world. It had been a wonderful night spent with the love of her life. They spent the rest of the day fixing up their backroom at Momma and Johnny's house. Although Anne Marie hated Johnny, she felt safe there as long as Cliff was with her. They giggled and teased as they hung posters on their walls. One large poster was of Kiss, Cliff's favorite band.

Their happiness was short lived. Not even a week passed when Johnny walked in their room and demanded the posters be taken down. "They were evil," he said. Cliff and Johnny got in a big argument and soon Anne Marie was packing to move to Pappy and Granny's. Johnny had tried to push Cliff around because Cliff was only sixteen. They soon became emancipated, which gave them the rights of adults even though they were under age. They were still trying to go to school. Cliff was a junior in high school and Anne Marie a freshman. Cliff would come to see her at lunch time.

After one of Cliff's visit to see Anne Marie, the principal called Anne Marie into his office. He informed her that Cliff couldn't come see her at school anymore. He said Anne Marie's parents could come see her, but Cliff could not. Anne Marie stood seething in his office. She glared at him and said, "Then you can take this school and shove it where the sun don't shine. I'm married, and my parents have no say about what I do. I'm out of here." Christmas break was beginning, and Annie Marie never returned to school.

The ninth grade was as far as Ann Marie attended high school. Cliff quit school as well, and they moved in with Poppa and Granny. Anne Marie was happy there. She felt safe. Poppa helped them get an old car to drive. He was a mechanic, and he had taken in an old Pontiac Lamans, and it was primer gray. Anne Marie felt so happy. They had a car, and she was safe. She set about to make a home for her husband.

Poppa and Granny owned an old rent house, which at the time was vacant. Granny suggested to Anne Marie that maybe they should move in to that house and have a place of their own. Anne Marie told Cliff about the house, and they happily accepted the offer and moved in to their first home together. They would party some and smoke a little pot.

Anne Marie worked at a pet store and decided she would buy Cliff a baby Boa. Cliff was so excited about his gift, and he built the snake a big cage with a glass front. They named her Medussa. They had accumulated a fish tank filled with bass and catfish, and they had rats to feed the snake. The house was really a dump, and when it rained, the water poured in; but they were young, and they were happy. Soon Anne Marie was pregnant.

In the days that followed, Anne Marie miscarried. At the time, she was crushed. She wanted that baby. But God must have known at that time in life, Anne Marie and Cliff didn't need a baby. They were drinking and smoking pot almost daily with Cliff's friends. One day, they decided they would load up Pappy's old station wagon with all the band's sound equipment and head to the woods close to Granny and Poppa's place. They could play as loud as they wanted out there. They smoked a little pot before they left, and it took them forever to get there. They were driving about 30 miles an hour, but to them, high on pot, it seemed like they were flying. Anne Marie kept telling the driver to get out of the ditch. He would swerve the car and then run into the ditch again. This went on and on. Finally, they arrived at their destination and got all the equipment unloaded only to discover no one brought extension cords, so they had no electricity. This was the beginning of a lifetime of addiction for pot and alcohol. It became a daily practice to smoke some pot and have a drink. In Anne Marie's words, she never just drank. When she drank, she intended to get drunk.

Later, Anne Marie and Cliff decided to trade the old car they had for a van. It was really a cool van. It had carpet inside on the walls. One side of the van had desert pictures, the other side had pictures of a night sky, all made out of carpet. Medussa the boa, loved to lay on the rack behind the driver's seat. Cliff liked to take her to the mall with him and watch people's faces when they saw him with this snake wrapped around his neck.

Anne Marie didn't go to Momma's house very often any more. Johnny still lived there, and she didn't want to see or talk to him. So when she went, she made sure he was gone or working. Anne Marie missed her Momma and her siblings dreadfully. One day, she went over for a visit and was helping Momma cook dinner. Her assignment was to defrost a package of frozen ribs. The knife halted midway through, trying to pry the ribs apart. Anne Marie pushed hard, and her hand slipped off the handle. She cut her little finger to the bone. Momma rushed her to the emergency room where a doctor looked at it and tried to assess the damage done to the finger.

The doctor thought Anne Marie was faking the extent of the injury as she couldn't bend the finger. He took a pin and probed the wound. Anne Marie told him she couldn't feel anything. He pulled the finger straight and stitched it up. Later, Anne Marie had to go to an orthopedic hand doctor where it was discovered that she had severed the tendon in the finger. Surgery followed, and in weeks, Anne Marie's hand was totally healed. But her taste for drugs only increased.

Following her surgery, Anne Marie was rummaging through an old shed behind their house. She discovered Granny had lots of antique furniture stored there. Some of it looked really nice. So she decided she needed to sell some of it for cash so she and Cliff could party. She pulled the old bed from the shed with Cliff's help, and they hauled it to an antique store. The owner bought the bed, and that night, Anne Marie and Cliff and a few of their friends had a pot and alcohol party at Granny's expense.

Anne Marie never realized how much that bed had meant to Granny until she saw how brokenhearted her grandmother was when she discovered the bed was gone. Anne Marie never confessed to taking the bed, but in her heart, she felt Granny knew what had happened. She never got to make amends with Granny about the bed, and she felt terrible. They had given her so much, and she repaid them by stealing from them. This became just another excuse to get drunk and forget about the whole thing.

4

The longer Anne Marie stayed away from Johnny, the better she felt. But the memories of him never left her mind. She often thought of the day Johnny decided he needed to cut her Doberman's ears into a point. He took the dog from Anne Marie's arms and proceeded to scissor off the dog's ears. The dog was yelping and whining as blood ran from his cropped ears. Anne Marie was crying and pleading with Johnny to stop. He didn't stop until he had cut the dog's ears into a bloody point. Anne Marie recalled the dog looked like a devil dog. Seemed only fitting since the devil himself had done the shaping.

As a child, Anne Marie had no way of knowing that animal cruelty was a sure sign of mental illness. That knowledge wouldn't have helped her with Johnny's animal abuse, but it might have helped others who were witness to his attacks. One day, he brought home a horse. Since Anne Marie was the animal lover in the family, of course it was hers. Johnny wanted the horse broke, so he saddled him up one day and climbed on board. The horse threw him off each time he tried to ride. It finally ended with Johnny taking a 2×4 and beating the animal over the head. Anne Marie knew what it was like to be on the receiving end of one of Johnny's beatings. The next day, he traded the horse for a shotgun. Anne Marie's heart broke as she watched Cheerios, her beautiful Palomino horse, hauled off in a horse trailer.

Johnny worked for a company that had a large stock tank. His family was allowed to go there and fish and in the summertime, go swimming. One day in late March, Anne Marie, her best friend Fae and some of her cousins, were having a family get together. One of the young cousins hit a ball, and it went flying into the stock tank. Anne Marie was on the dock, and she reached for the ball when it hit the water. The more she tried to retrieve the ball, the farther out it would go. Suddenly, Anne Marie fell into the cold March waters of the huge stock tank. Her tennis shoes immediately became water logged and kept pulling her under. She could look up and see the light on top of the water, but try as she might, there was no surfacing. Anne Marie's momma couldn't swim, but realizing Anne Marie was going to drown if she didn't do something, she jumped in and was able to grab Anne Marie's plaid flannel shirt. She dog paddled her way to the dock with Anne Marie in tow. That day for the first time, Anne Marie realized God had been with her. In the years that followed, Anne Marie would recall that day of terror and wonder why God had spared her life.

When Anne Marie was in the sixth grade, she and her friend Fae decided they would take their lunch money and buy cigarettes. The first time they smoked one, they coughed and wheezed until they thought they would surely die; but with time and practice, they became pretty good at it. Johnny caught her smoking and told her if she was going to smoke, she had to buy her own cigarettes. From then on, Anne Marie would light up in front of anyone. She would take a deep pull and the trail of blue smoke she blew from her mouth was a sign of an accomplished smoker at the age of thirteen.

Momma started having severe headaches. She called them migraines, but they were so severe she would pass out. Anne Marie would see that someone took her to the emergency room, but usually, all they did was give her a shot for pain and send her home. On one of these rushed trips to the hospital, they were fortunate enough to encounter a doctor on duty who took an interest in Momma and listened to their story. He examined her and immediately had her sent to Baylor in Dallas. When she arrived, a team of surgeons were waiting, and they did emergency surgery on Momma. She had an aneurysm behind her left eye. The doctors told the family that Momma was a miracle because she died during surgery, and they were able to revive her. Granny, who was a nurse, stayed by Momma day and night until she recovered. But because Momma was gone, the kids had to stay home with Johnny. Because Anne Marie was the oldest, she had to do the cooking, cleaning, and babysit her younger siblings. When Momma finally got to come home, Johnny would make fun of her because she had her head shaved. He would tell her she wasn't all there after the surgery. Recollection told Anne Marie the reason he thought that was because Momma finally started standing up for herself, something she had never done before.

Momma never got the courage to leave Johnny and stay gone. She always went back to him sooner or later. Anne

Marie hated Johnny for the way he treated Momma and what he was doing to her, but she never had the courage to tell on him until that fateful day when she was fourteen and had all of Johnny she was going to take. The sad fact was by this time, Anne Marie thought nothing of having sex with anyone. It became as natural as breathing, and she learned at an early age, sex could help her get what she wanted. Sex, alcohol, and drugs were now a constant in Anne Marie's life.

Johnny often accused Anne Marie of doing things that she was innocent of. However, in time, she thought if she was going to be punished, she might as well do the deed. Rachel, her younger sister, however, did do everything Anne Marie had been accused of. She would slip out of the house and take the car. On one occasion, she and her boyfriend were flying down the road in the family car and hit a bridge. Anne Marie reflected on that day and in her memory, could still hear Momma crying when the doctors told her Rachel was not going to survive. What they didn't know was the determination of this young person when she decides she's going to live. Rachel was a fighter, and soon she was out of the ICU ward and on the floor as a regular patient. The doctors once again predicted Rachel would never walk, but she again proved them wrong. The day Rachel walked in the front door of her home with bars sticking out of her pelvis and hips just to hold them together, made Anne Maries heart sink. But as time passed, Rachel healed; and one more time, God blessed this dysfunctional family.

This time, she was determined to have this baby and not miscarry. She did no drugs and smoked no pot for the nine months she carried her precious cargo. She prayed she would have a little girl that looked exactly like Cliff. The downside of the pregnancy was Anne Marie gained seventy pounds. When her time to deliver came, she watched as the days stretched into weeks. Two weeks past her due date and still no baby. Old wives' tales said that if she drank castor oil, it would cause her to go into labor. She downed a big dose, and Cliff took her walking over hills and trails, but still no baby. Finally, the doctor had Anne Marie check into the hospital; and the next day, Anne Marie delivered the most beautiful baby girl she had ever laid eyes upon. At seventeen, she had become a mother with no idea of what mothers were supposed to do. She counted all the baby's fingers and toes and marveled at this perfect being she held so tightly in her teenage arms. The next chapter in Anne Marie's life had begun.

5

Cliff and Anne Marie named the baby Amelia after Cliff's Granny. When Amelia was three months old, Anne Marie's Aunt Betty gave her a baby shower. Anne Marie had never seen so much baby stuff. Little ruffled dresses and panties to match. There were blankets, diapers, and toiletries of all kind. And best of all, Anne Marie's art teacher, Ms. Williams, attended. Ms. Williams was Anne Marie's favorite teacher, and she had taken Ms. Williams as her role model. She was a very attractive lady, and Anne Marie's Uncle Todd hit on her the whole time while she was at the baby shower. He was drunk, and Anne Marie was embarrassed. She often wondered why her family couldn't be just normal instead of always being an embarrassment to her. Anne Marie had won a gold medal under the guidance of Ms. Williams and her art class. But the gold medal was soon forgotten as Cliff and Anne Marie loaded up all the baby things they had received and took them home.

The backroom of Granny and Poppa's house soon became very crowded with the baby bed and all the baby stuff that was required. Anne Marie shuffled everything around every day, trying to find just one more inch of room. One day, Cliff came home from work and announced his real father had contacted him. The bewilderment on Cliff's face told Anne Marie he wasn't quite sure how to handle the situation. There had been a picture of Cliff and the baby along with Cliff's Granny and Pappy showing five generations of Moore's. Somehow, Cliff's daddy had seen the picture and realized Cliff was his son. His name was Bill Blankenship, and he was a multimillionaire, or at least Anne Marie thought he was.

In the days that followed the meeting of Mr. Blankenship, Anne Marie and Cliff enjoyed the bounty the newly found father produced. The first time Blankenship saw Amelia, he gave Cliff and Anne Marie $300 and told them to buy something for the baby. Then he told them to take his new Lincoln Continental to town along with his credit card and buy them some water skis. They were all going skiing on his new fifty-two-foot Sea Ray boat with its two Corvette engines. When Anne Marie was seated in the passenger side of the Lincoln, she looked around in bewilderment. She had never been in such a fine car, and it even smelled new. She glanced out the window of the car and saw Cliff's dad with his arm around this beautiful blonde. Anne Marie found out later this young blonde was Blankenship's wife. In the weeks and months that followed, Anne Marie and Cliff would join Cliff's father every time he came to town. On such occasions, Blankenship encouraged Cliff to join the military and learn a trade. Cliff refused to cut his hair, and he loved music, so no way was he giving that up. The relationship between Cliff and his father became a long distance affair except on the rare occasion when Cliff's father came to town.

Anne Marie still had horrible nightmares about Johnny. She prayed they would end, but they never did. She realized too late that she should have taken the counselor's offer back when she first filed charges against Johnny. They had offered to set her up with a counselor, and perhaps in talking about it aloud, it would start the healing process. Anne Marie refused then, and she sure didn't intend to pick it up now, so the nightmares continued. So did the drugs and alcohol.

While spending time with his father, Cliff was encouraged to cut his hair and join the military to learn a trade. Not wishing to leave the lifestyle of long hair and music, Cliff had refused. But as the days and months stretched out before him, his father's voice kept ringing in his ears to join the military and learn a trade. He made his decision and tried to figure a way to tell Anne Marie so that she wouldn't totally go off the deep end.

Anne Marie had been acting so jealous in the past months that Cliff was often on the receiving end of her jealous tirades. If a girl so much as whispered a song request, Anne Marie saw it as a direct threat to their relationship. Cliff, on the other hand, knew that Anne Marie suffered from low self-esteem, and the excess weight she had put on during her pregnancy was not helping matters. So with reluctance, he told Anne Marie of his plans to join the Navy.

At first, Anne Marie burst into tears and started shouting that he was only doing that to get away from her and the baby. She accused Cliff of everything she could think of and finally collapsed in an exhausted heap on the couch. Cliff took advantage of Anne Marie's silence and told her of all the plans he had for them, but he explained he had to get some sort of education and learn a trade, or the dreams they shared would never happen.

Cliff gently wiped the tears from Anne Marie's eyes while declaring the love he had for her. Finally, Anne Marie agreed to the plan. She and Amelia would continue to live with Cliff's grandparents as he went away to the Navy.

Anne Marie watched as Cliff embarked on an airplane headed for boot camp in the Great Lake area. She fought back the creeping fear that he was actually leaving the baby and her and would never return. Anne Marie had never been away from Cliff since their marriage, and the loneliness she felt reached the depths of her very being. She ached for Cliff's presence. She had placed him on some kind of pedestal in her mind. He was her hero. He had rescued her from Johnny; now she was left alone to find her own way.

The days and nights Anne Marie and Amelia spent with Granny and Pappy stretched into months. Anne Marie wrote Cliff daily, filling the blank spaces of her letter with descriptions of things the baby had done, or what she was learning to do. After the baby went to sleep at night, Anne Marie would puff on pot and drink until she passed out.

A few days before Cliff's graduation from boot camp, the Navy found out about his pot and drug use. He washed out of the program he had so wanted to obtain. The Navy asked him to go work with the chaplain, but Cliff refused. Instead, he packed up his belongings and headed home. His getting into the electronic program aboard a nuclear submarine rested on his background check, but once his drug use came out, the Navy wanted nothing more to do with Cliff. The hopes that he had for himself and his small family went up in a puff of blue smoke.

Anne Marie was overjoyed that Cliff was home. It didn't matter to her that he had washed out of the program. She worshipped the ground he walked on, and just to have him home was enough for her. They moved into a small apartment behind a large house. The garage apartment was barely big enough for their bed and Amelia's baby bed. As usual, they had extra guests. Two of the band members stayed there all the time. That made the small space smaller, and privacy became a wished-upon might-have-been.

Rachel had received a settlement for the horrible wreck she and her boyfriend had. It was a large settlement, and Rachel was generous with the money. She would buy a quarter pound of pot and bring it over and share with Anne Marie, Cliff, and the two band members. They would all light up, and the smoke would be so thick you could hardly see. Anne Marie loved the way the pot made her feel. She soon learned that if Amelia cried and couldn't sleep, all she had to do was put her in the car, roll up the windows, and puff away. Soon Amelia would be high and go to sleep. This was just the beginning for Amelia. Before she would turn five, she would have been high on alcohol and weed and have the ability to cuss like a sailor.

One night in late December, Anne Marie, her sister Rachel, husband, Cliff, and two band members, were engrossed in a pot party. Rachel had once again furnished the pot, and all were smoking down when a knock sounded at the front door. A policeman stood in the entrance as Cliff opened the door, and a room full of marijuana smoke greeted the surprised visitor. He was looking for a runaway, or so he said. Having seen immediately what was going on, he came in and relieved the surprised partiers of their cache of pot. He promptly flushed it down the toilet. Anne

Marie later recalled with laughter how funny Cliff and the others looked, dipping what they could salvage from the porcelain pot, and placing it on a cookie sheet to dry in the oven. They saved enough to finish their night of partying. The next morning, they all awoke and started all over again.

6

Cliff started his sentence with, "I've never been with another woman. I married you when I was sixteen, and I wonder what another woman would be like."

Anne Marie just looked at him. He spoke the truth, and maybe if she agreed, he would see she was the best, and the thought of another would leave his mind. Of course, she arrived at that decision through a cloud of alcohol and pot. Any decision she made would be clouded. "Well if that will make you happy, then go for it." That's all Anne Marie said, and then she went about to talk her best friend at the time into sleeping with Cliff. Of course, the whole escapade ended in total chaos with Anne Marie furious with Cliff, running her best friend off, and feeling totally dejected and alone. That one decision affected their marriage for years to come. Anne Marie lost her best friend, and Cliff had fallen off the pedestal Anne Marie had placed him on. After she sobered up, she wanted to vomit every time she looked at Cliff. He was disgusting to her.

But it was a good excuse to stay drunk all time. It never occurred to Anne Marie that she was as much to blame for the incident as Cliff was. It was the beginning of the end of their marriage.

Anne Marie got a job at a nearby convenience store. In order to be closer to her work, they moved close to the lake. Anne Marie liked working, but most of all, she loved getting off work and going home where she was greeted by three band members, Cliff, and her baby. The band members might as well have lived with them because they never went home, and every night was a repeat of the night before. When she got home, everybody was ready to party, and party they did. Anne Marie would drink till she passed out and then get up the next morning and go to work.

In spite of her nights of partying, Anne Marie was good at her job. She always carded the people to be sure she never sold alcohol to an underage person. However, one night, a young man came in that she remembered carding before. He bought a six pack and Anne Marie smiled and said, "You come back," as she handed him his change. He got out the front door, and Anne Marie looked up to see two policemen entering the store. She greeted them, and their reply shocked her, "Ma'am, you're under arrest for selling alcohol to a minor."

Anne Marie couldn't believe her ears. "What are you talking about? I have carded him before. He's not a minor."

"Oh, but he is, and you just sold him alcohol."

For the first time in her life, Anne Marie was arrested and carried to jail. She was nineteen and scared to death. As she stared at the gray walls of the cell, she became angry. She hadn't been allowed to call Cliff to bail her out. He thought she was at work. Anne Marie started pounding on the bars and screaming, "When do I get my phone call?" She was answered with silence.

It seemed like days to Anne Marie when in actuality, it was only hours before Cliff showed up to get her out of jail. She collapsed into his arms, and anger and fear came rolling out.

"Can you believe these idiots?" Anne Marie screamed. "I had carded that guy a dozen times before. I knew he was not a minor."

"Anne Marie, shut up," Cliff commanded. "Wait until we get in the car unless you want to spend another four hours locked up."

Fortunately for Anne Marie, her boss didn't fire her. She believed her when she told what happened.

"You have to always be careful, Anne Marie, when you're selling alcohol. You never know when the cops are setting you up just to see if the establishment would sell to a minor. That's a serious offense and can carry a stiff penalty."

"I know that's true," Anne Marie replied. "I'll never do that again."

Anne Marie's brief encounter with police and jail was a preview of her life to come.

The minute they got home, the party began, and soon Anne Marie was so high she forgot about her jail encounter.

During the session of taking shots of tequila and chasing it with a shot of vodka, someone in the party slipped Anne Marie a hit of acid. Anne Marie went crazy. She was running around the house in nothing but a T-shirt and panties. She cussed and tore things up, and it took three grown men to subdue her enough to place her in a shower to try and cool her off. They succeeded in pissing Anne Marie off even more, and she ripped at their clothes; and finally, Cliff, in desperation, called his mom to come and see if she could help calm Anne Marie down. At daybreak, Anne Marie finally collapsed from exhaustion and went to sleep. She didn't find out what had happened to her until years later. She thought she had just been drunk.

The events that followed that night of madness were equally disturbing. They had obtained an old car that would start only after it was pushed down the hill and the clutch popped. Not knowing how to pop the clutch, Anne Marie volunteered to always push the car. On this particular day, she thought it would be neat to jump on the trunk of the car and ride down the hill. She didn't realize when Cliff popped the clutch, the car would lurch forward. When it did, it threw Anne Marie to the ground. She lay there stunned until Cliff ran back to see about her. He helped her to her feet, and she noticed her wrist was dangling at an odd angle. She realized it was broken, and the other arm was too painful to even lift. A trip to the emergency room revealed that ligaments in her arm were torn, and the wrist was broken. The nurse commented about how pitiful she looked with one arm in a sling and the other wrist in a cast. All Anne Marie wanted to do was throw up. If it hadn't been for a hog's leg they had in their possession, the pain would have been overpowering. A few drags on the marijuana kept the pain somewhat abated, until she could get some of the good drugs in her system.

The injury to her arms only gave Anne Marie a very good excuse to stay high on pot and alcohol while she recovered. The fights between her and Cliff had been taking place with increasing occurrence. When they both were drunk, the meanness came out, and harsh words were spoken between them. But it was Anne Marie's escape from reality, and that was exactly what she wanted. Not to think about anything. Anne Marie would get in Cliff's face and hit him hard. Even though he was a big man, he never hit her back. He would just push her out of the way or throw her on the bed. He would just defend himself against her blows and try not to let her get close enough to bite him, which she always did if given the chance. His defense of himself only made Anne Marie's rage escalate.

One night, Cliff was at band practice, and Anne Marie started in on him. She became so angry she picked up the microphone and flung it at him. Fortunately, the bottom iron stand missed his head by inches. Anne Marie always felt horrible about her actions when she sobered up, but sobriety never lasted very long. During one of their bouts of fighting, Anne Marie met a man who frequented the store where she was a cashier. He was always saying nice things to her, and she went out with him even though she knew he was married, and they had sex. Anne Marie confessed her affair to Cliff one night just for spite. She wanted him to know what it felt like to have the one you love sleep with another, just as he had done. She wanted Cliff to be as miserable as she was. Not long after her confession, Cliff and Anne Marie separated.

7

So now what? Anne Marie thought to herself. *I'm separated from my husband, I have a baby to raise, and I want to party. What am I supposed to do?*

All these thoughts raced through Anne Marie's mind, but in honesty, she really didn't care about anything but getting high. She had found a good babysitter to look after Amelia while she partied. The rest of life didn't matter.

One day, she got a call from her mother. Her mother said she was divorcing Johnny. "Well," came Anne Marie's reply, "It's about damn time."

"Well, he hit your baby sister, and I am sick of his abuse, so I'm divorcing him," Anne Marie's mother explained.

You got to be kidding me, Anne Marie thought. *Rachel and I endured sexual as well as physical abuse from his hands, yet he slaps baby sister and Momma leaves. Go figure that one out.*

Soon after Momma's announcement she was divorcing Johnnie, she also announced she was moving to Galveston. Anne Marie had never been away from her family, so she decided she would move to Galveston as well. She packed up Amelia's clothes as well as her own and told the guy she was living with she was moving to Galveston. He decided he would move also, so they packed up all their belonging, and the dysfunctional family once again landed in a different city. If Anne Marie thought she would leave her problems behind by changing cities where she lived, she was sadly mistaken. She soon discovered that sins of the past simply follow you to whatever residence you find. Once settled in a new town, old habits surfaced, and she found she could get as high there as she could anywhere. The lies she told herself worked as they always had so time and circumstance made no difference.

Momma would drag Anne Marie's siblings back to the town they had left about two or three times a month. Anne Marie would tag along only to find that each time she went back to her old surroundings, she found Cliff's memory never very far from her mind. Anne Marie would sit with her head in her hands and cry for the love of her life and their life together. She made up her mind. She would tell Cliff whatever he needed to hear in order to get her life back with him.

After much negotiating and talking, Cliff and Annie Marie got back together. Anne Marie didn't bother to tell the guy she had been living with that she was leaving Galveston. She was afraid he would try and stop her, so she just left him and their apartment and everything she had moved there and moved back in with Cliff. She lay in his arms that first night and felt truly safe and happy to be back home. In Annie Marie's twisted mind, she felt that Cliff could and would once again save her from herself.

During the reunion of their time together, they lived with Cliff's grandparents, Pappy and Granny. They continued to drink and party every chance they got. On one weekend, Annie Marie's little sister Maddie came to spend the night with them. Maddie was young and had never been high. She was curious, so Annie Marie and friends decided it would be great sport to get Maddie high. They gladly fixed her up with all the alcohol she would swallow, and soon Maddie was rolling around on the floor so drunk she couldn't stand, with the onlookers roaring with laughter. Annie Marie knew Maddie was totally out of control and felt bad she had allowed this to happen to her little sister. She handcuffed Maddie to her bed so she could keep an eye on her and let her sleep it off. The next day, Maddie had no memory of the previous night's events. She just knew she never wanted another drink of alcohol. Annie Marie reasoned that perhaps that was the best thing that could have happened to her. And perhaps it was.

After a night of partying and smoking pot, Anne Marie would often be awakened by Amelia's screams. She would ask her what's wrong, and Amelia would tell her there were monsters in her room with big glasses and purple hair. Anne Marie reasoned it was the after effects of the baby inhaling too much marijuana smoke and draining all the alcohol glasses on the coffee table. They often would take the baby for a ride if she was whining and crying and roll up the car window and light up a joint. Soon the baby would get the secondhand smoke and go to sleep. These were shameful nights and days for Annie Marie, and not once did she think that Child protective services could come in and take her baby away.

At the keg parities in their home, Cliff and Annie Marie would invite all their friends, and some of them would ride their motorcycles into the house and kick holes in the walls.

Anne Marie and Cliff didn't mind because they were even higher than their guests. The next morning, Anne Marie would awake to a house full of beer cans and dirty floors. There was never any food in the house, and she would have to go to a grocery store and steal some lunch meat and scrape together enough change to buy bread. Amelia was hungry, and Anne Marie found ways to feed her, but Annie Marie always had enough money to get high or drunk.

During this time, the wife of one of their drinking buddies would come over and take Amelia home with her. She didn't want child protective custody to take the child, so she would keep her until Anne Marie and Cliff sobered up. The lady's husband would drink with Anne Marie and Cliff while his wife babysits. Anne Marie was glad to have free babysitting and not have to worry about the Amelia. The lady's name was Ann, and she turned out to be a very positive influence on Anne Marie's and Cliff's lives.

Ann would witness to them every chance she got about Jesus and the many wonderful things he had done for her. Ann's husband, Greg, became Anne Marie's drinking buddy, and Anne Marie grew to love him like a father. It was a strange friendship. Ann would preach the gospel to Anne Marie and Cliff while Greg would drink with them. But at least for the moment, Amelia was safe.

One weekend, Anne Marie and Cliff decided they would visit the church Ann had started in the bedroom of her home. They arrived at the house and were warmly welcomed by Ann. She led them to the bedroom, and after they all were comfortably seated, she started telling them about Jesus. In one of these worship services, Ann gave a book to Annie Marie that would forever change her life. It was called Rapture, and it spoke of the last days on earth before the Lord returned. The book scared the hell out of Anne Marie because she knew if the Lord returned at that moment, she would forever be lost to Satan and his wicked ways. She knew she would be condemned to burn in hell for eternity. Anne Marie knew she didn't want that for herself or Cliff, but what could she do about it? She started questioning Ann and getting answers straight from the Bible. Anne Marie studied and soon she and Cliff knelt beside Ann's bed and invited Jesus into their life and asked forgiveness for their sins. Before long, all their friends started attending that meager little church Ann had started in her home, and they quickly outgrew Ann's house. They worked as a unified group to find another meeting place for the small flock and were rewarded with more room and space in an old grocery store front.

The little congregation grew, and they witnessed to all those they had partied with, telling them about Jesus and his wonderful forgiveness and the peace that came from following him. Amelia grew, and for the first time in their marriage, Anne Marie and Cliff were truly happy. Ann's husband, Greg, had also been saved, and they were like one big happy family. No more boisterous weekends with drunks and dope addicts, but peaceful gatherings with sober folks. Anne Marie witnessed that Jesus was better than any drug or alcohol she had ever had.

The Lord started dealing with Anne Marie about forgiveness. She knew she had to forgive Johnny if she was to ever be totally free of him and the wrong things he had done to her, her siblings, and her momma. But forgiveness came hard, and Annie Marie fought. She hated him and everything he stood for. It was too painful to go back and recall all that had happened to her at Johnny's hand, but the

Lord instructed her that she had to forgive so she could get on with her life.

Anne Marie wanted another baby. Amelia was almost five, and Anne Marie thought that would be perfect for a little boy baby. She wanted him to have blonde hair and blue eyes, and that's what she prayed for. God granted her wish, and once again, Anne Marie was pregnant. She wanted the baby to look like her because Amelia looked exactly like Cliff, and so Anne Marie anxiously awaited the birth of their baby.

When the baby was born, Anne Marie counted all his toes and fingers and examined him head to toe. He was perfect. God had blessed Cliff and her once again with a healthy baby. Even the nurses commented that they had never seen hair that golden and eyes that blue. He was exactly what Anne Marie had prayed for. They welcomed Jacob into their family with thanksgiving. Life was good. Anne Marie was happy. But tragedy lurked around the corner, and once again Satan would attempt to destroy her.

8

Ann and Greg worked part-time making fishing lures. They taught all the members of the church who wanted to learn how to make some really exotic and beautiful lures. Greg would then take them out and sell them to different stores. Anne Marie got very good at making the fishing lures, and every morning, Greg would come by to pick up the lures, have a cup of coffee, and say good morning. Anne Marie looked forward to these visits. She had come to idolize Greg and loved him more than she had ever loved her real father. Greg was good to her and her family, and his good-natured manner was always uplifting to Anne Marie. Cliff was now the song leader at their church, and Cliff's band had replaced their rock and roll music with songs of praise for the Lord. Greg never failed to remind Anne Marie how blessed she was to have her two beautiful children and a husband as gifted as Cliff. Then he would hug her and the children and be out the door rejoicing for another day.

One particular morning, Greg sat and talked a little longer than usual. It was almost as though he didn't want to leave. Anne Marie was happy to just sit and visit with him. They talked about how the church had grown, and he picked up both Amelia and Jacob and gave them a big hug. Then he picked up the fishing lures Anne Marie had so painstakingly made and walked out the door and out of Anne Marie's life forever.

Anne Marie dropped the phone on the floor and slid down the wall in disbelief. The voice on the other end of the telephone told her that after Greg left her house that morning, he was involved in an automobile accident. Ironically, a drunk had hit him, and he died instantly. One more time, Anne Marie had lost someone she loved. One more time, disbelief crowded her mind.

The next few days were nothing but a blur to Anne Marie. The funeral service, the burial of her very best friend, was more than she could handle. She tried telling herself that Greg was with Jesus, and that he was happy, but that was no comfort to Anne Marie. She hugged Ann and their children and heard herself speak words of comfort to them, but she found no comfort for herself. Anne Marie was bitter. Why would God take the one man in her life she loved like her father? Why would he leave her once again with a feeling of abandonment? What was she supposed to do now? For several months after Greg's tragic passing, Cliff and Annie Marie attended church every Sunday. The crowd grew smaller and smaller, and finally the church doors closed.

For a short period of time, Anne Marie and Cliff went to another church; but no matter where she was, the spirit of Greg would surround her, and finally Anne Marie quit going to church at all. With each passing day, Anne Marie grew angrier with God. How could he allow this to happen to her just as her life had gotten so good? How could this loving God hurt her so badly?

She would go out in the woods and shout and cuss and look upward toward heaven as if she was looking God in the face. She didn't care what anyone thought; she would show this Almighty God just how pissed off she was at him. The irony of it all was that Anne Marie had often wondered how anyone who said they loved God could turn their back on him. She was finding out that could be done real easy when someone's heart is broken.

Anne Marie wandered around in a daze the first year Greg was gone. She started going over to Pappy and Granny's and helping them clean house and do odd jobs. Pappy always had a fifth of whiskey in the pantry, and Anne Marie started taking shots of it to get a buzz going. Then she would go home and try to act civilized toward her husband. Cliff was working nights now, and that made it harder and harder for Anne Marie to talk to him. He would sleep all day while she and the kids were up, and then he went to work when they were asleep. Anne Marie and Cliff started drifting further and further apart. Anne Marie would openly light up a joint against Cliff's protest. She didn't really care whether he liked it or not.

One of the band members started coming over and smoking a joint with her at night. They would set out on the front porch after Anne Marie put the kids down for the night and visit. It felt good to have an adult to talk to, and so it began. Anne Marie knew not to mention to Cliff that Al the band member was coming over. She knew Cliff would not stand for that, so she just didn't tell him. Every now and then, Anne Marie would stop over at Al's house and visit with him. One fateful night, she made the mistake of going to bed with him. She never did understand why she did that. She tried to lie to herself and say it was just because she was lonely, but she knew better. She did it because she wanted to, and that was all there was to that. He certainly didn't mean anything to her, but heck he was handy; and she was willing, and so the deceit and lies began again.

When Jacob started kindergarten, Anne Marie enrolled in college. She wanted to become a nurse like her grandmother. She had gotten her GED by the time she was nineteen, so all she had to do was study, take care of the kids, and go to school. Two years after she enrolled in a junior college, she received her associate's degree in science. She needed two more years to become an RN, but Anne Marie was tired, and her life was back in shambles, so she decided she would just quit school and rest for awhile. She and Cliff were arguing all the time about something. On his days off, Cliff would have band practice, so there was never any time for the family. He hardly noticed when Anne Marie would light up a joint and follow it with a shot of whiskey. He spent a lot of time on the computer, and the next thing, Anne Marie discovered Cliff and some girl he met on line were going out. That was it for Anne Marie. She packed up what little belongings she had and moved out. One of the things she got was a Smith and Wesson Model 41 pistol.

Anne Marie left Jacob and Amelia with Cliff. *Why not?* she reasoned to herself. He was by far the better care giver. He hadn't started back drinking and smoking pot like she had, so in her heart, she knew the kids were better off with Cliff. That didn't make it any easier. She felt like her heart was being torn right out of her chest each time she lift Jacob and Amelia, especially when Jacob would cry and say he didn't understand why she couldn't stay home like she used to.

Anne Marie felt as though there was nothing left to live far. One night, she put the Smith and Wesson Model 41 pistol in her mouth. With tears streaming down her face, she glanced up and saw the pictures of Amelia and Jacob. She removed the pistol from her mouth and put it in a drawer. She couldn't take her life and leave her children. She soon sold the gun back to Cliff. She started drinking more and more to wash away the memories and not feel the pain.

She stayed high most of the time. She didn't try to hide it anymore. Her visits to see her children became further and further apart. She reasoned they were better off without her anyway, so why let them see her in the state of total drunkenness. Anne Marie was quickly becoming that person she had always hated. She was now a full-blown alcoholic like Johnny. Church and God seemed far away now to her, and that was just the way she liked it.

Momma had a job at a local lodge. She had worked herself up to a supervisor, so naturally, Anne Marie hit her up for a job. She got Anne Marie a job as a chambermaid. Each day Anne Marie changed the bed linens on all the cottage cabins that were rented. It was hard work, but Anne Marie liked it because she didn't have to think much. Just strip the beds and remake them, pretty routine. On one of the rum-dum days, Anne Marie met a guy named Bruce. Bruce was younger than Anne Marie, and he became totally smitten with her. Perhaps he'd never been with a woman before that was quite as worldly as Anne Marie, but whatever the reason, they soon moved in together. This was also about the time Anne Marie discovered mini-thins. If she took the mini-thins and chased it with alcohol, she could really get a buzz on. Her daily routine consisted of shots of tequila with a beer chaser, mini-thins and smoking pot. She never allowed herself to sober up. However, she could function in that state. Why not, she'd been that way a long time.

When Momma tried to talk some sense into Anne Marie, she would laugh at her and say, "Oh, please, Momma, give me a break. You of all people do not need to be preaching to me."

One Christmas, the lodge threw a big Christmas bash. All the employees were invited, and so Anne Marie and Bruce were in attendance. Both were pretty well too drunk to know what was going on, when a guy made a pass at Anne Marie. Bruce was insanely jealous, so he immediately confronted the guy. Anne Marie didn't want her bosses to see how drunk she and Bruce were, and she especially didn't want them to witness a free-for-all brawl. Anne Marie started coaxing Bruce toward the door; she felt she had to get him outside before he wrecked the place, and they both lose their job. Just as they stepped out the door, Anne Marie lost her balance and fell in the bushes. Bruce tried to help her up but ran into the brick wall and dislocated his shoulder. It was obvious Bruce needed medical attention, so Anne Marie told him she would drive him to the hospital. She knew she was way too drunk to be driving, but if she closed one eye, she could see three images. She picked the one in the middle to follow, and by the grace of God almighty, they made it to the emergency room. The waiting room was almost empty because of the early morning hour. Anne Marie waited until the doctors took Bruce back to the treatment room, and then she headed for the car to take a hit of pot. Trouble was, she couldn't find anyone with a light. She wandered around the parking lot hollering loudly for someone to give her a light. Finally, she just set down as the city police pulled up. They questioned Anne Marie and arrested her for public intoxication. She got to spend the night in the city jail.

One afternoon, Anne Marie and Bruce were at the lake, smoking pot and drinking. Anne Marie always had a dog of some kind. This day she had loaded up the dog and brought it with her to the lake. She would throw sticks in the water, and the dog would retrieve them. Bruce wanted her to talk to him and leave the dog alone. Anne Marie and her stubbornness refused to stop playing with the dog. Finally, Bruce caught the dog and made it yelp. Anne Marie flew into him like a fighting rooster; she slapped and kicked and beat the tar out of Bruce. In the ruckus, she hit him in his nose and broke it. Blood went all over both of them, but she didn't care. When they got home, she started packing her bags. She was leaving; she screamed at Bruce as he tried to stop her. Another fight broke out, and she shoved Bruce hard into the wall. He dislocated his shoulder again, and she made her getaway as Bruce lay on the ground withering with pain. That relationship was over.

Shortly after breaking up with Bruce, Anne Marie sobered up enough to get another job. She loved this job. It was at a movie rental house, and she learned to clean the movies and repackage them with shrink wrap. Some of her friends and her sister Rachel worked there too, so she got to see part of her family every day. She liked that. Working hard always came easy for her, and before long, they made her a supervisor. This was different for Anne Marie. She had never been responsible for other people. As a matter of fact, Anne Marie had not been responsible for herself.

She had gone and done what she wanted when she wanted and the thought of having to use her mind and help other people do their jobs scared her.

Perhaps the hiring of other people made Anne Marie feel insecure. Knowing it was her responsibility to put people who could be trusted and capable of doing the work that had to be done day in and day out, unnerved her the most. She was a sucker for a sob story. It seemed that everyone who came to interview for a job had a sob story to tell, and she fell for them all. This resulted in her having to do the job she had hired others to do because they fell down on their job and made her look bad to her bosses. It didn't take many months of this for her to smarten up and tell her boss that she no longer wanted a supervisory job. She just wanted to do her work and let everyone else do theirs. So that was her brief encounter with the upper echelons of a company. After that, she went to weekend bazaars and sold the movies. But time and circumstance forced her to feel that she needed another drink, and pretty soon she added a little speed to the mixture. Her life was totally out of control, and she couldn't care less.

"I need wheels, fast wheels, but cheap wheels," Anne Marie was talking to the car salesman.

The car salesman sized her up as he looked her up and down, then he said, "Step this way, lady. I've got the ride for you."

Anne Marie eyed the teal green Nissan pickup and then opened the door. It was clean enough inside, so she climbed in. Turning the key, the engine of the little truck responded instantly and sounded good as Anne Marie let it idle between bouts of riving it up. "How much?" Anne Marie asked.

"Just for you today, $3,000." The car salesman smiled. "Best bargain on the lot," he added.

"Well I want it detailed," Anne Marie stated.

"Of course, what day can you bring it back for that?"

"How about Monday morning?"

"Not a problem, come to the office, and let's make this little jewel yours." The salesman smiled as he helped Anne Marie out of the truck.

As the car salesman filled out the paperwork, Anne Marie fumbled around for the money. She had worked and stuffed money in every nook and cranny she could find until she had about $5,000 saved up. Unfortunately, her speed freak friends had found some of it and stolen it from her. She looked at the crumpled bills in her hands and thought about how lucky she was she had salvaged the $3,000. She plunked the crumpled money on the salesman's desk and set back in the chair and let out a big sigh of relief. Now she would have wheels that were hers alone. She wouldn't have to beg anyone for transportation. Her life had improved, and she was happy. But happiness would be short lived for her because the old devil had taken permanent residence in her life, and he refused to let her go.

Monday morning came quickly after a weekend of partying and drinking. Anne Marie climbed out of bed, got dressed, and made a feeble attempt to comb her hair. She was out the door and on her way to have her latest mode of transportation, cleaned up. She pulled in the drive, and the car salesman greeted her with his big cheesy smile and opened the door.

Anne Marie took the salesman's extended hand and shook hands with him as she asked, "Are you ready to detail this ride?"

The sales man nodded affirmative as he escorted her into his office. He called the service department and told them to come get the pickup and what to do. Then he turned to Anne Marie and said, "Would you like a drink?"

"At nine o'clock in the morning?" Anne Marie smiled. "Guess it's five o'clock somewhere. Give me a shot of that Crown Royal and a chaser of that tequila."

The car salesman and Anne Marie set in his office, and she had drink after drink. The hours rolled by, and soon Anne Marie was too drunk to drive. The car salesman asked where she wanted them to drive her, and she told them to her momma's house. That was the last thing she remembered until about five-thirty that afternoon.

Anne Marie woke with a start. She glanced out the window and saw that sundown was minutes away. *How in the name of God did I get here?* she wondered. She could hear her mother in the kitchen fixing supper. "Momma," she called.

"Yes," replied her mother.

"I've got to get out of here. I'm already late getting home, and it's getting dark."

"What's the matter? Doesn't your pickup have headlights?"

"Yeah, Momma, see you later," Anne Marie called as she darted out the door.

Anne Marie gunned the Nissan as she started up the hill to her house. She hit some loose gravel, and the next thing she knew, she was laying upside down in the ditch. Her head was still foggy from the Crown Royal and tequila, and it took her a minute to realize what had happened.

"Oh, no. I just got my pickup cleaned up, and it smells brand-new. Now I've wrecked it," Anne Marie said out loud to the darkness. She squirmed around and got the seatbelt unfastened as she tried to figure out how she was going to get out of the truck. The driver's side was next to the ground, and the passenger side window was facing the full moon that made it bright enough for Anne Marie to see how to get out of the truck.

Nothing's broke, she thought to herself. She lowered the passenger side window with the window crank and proceeded to climb out. She glanced around and saw no headlights of oncoming cars, so she jumped to the ground. A stabbing pain caused her to scream in response.

"Oh holy mother of God! Now what?" Anne Marie said out loud. She stared down at her ankle that was already swelling and looked as if it was broken. "This is great. I get out of a wrecked truck with no injuries and break my ankle trying to crawl out. This is just my luck."

Anne Marie looked around and realized her house was just up the hill, so she started hopping, trying to reach it. She looked back at her wrecked Nissan, and tears started rolling down her cheeks. Some of the tears were for her pain, and some were from the fact she knew she had lost her method of transportation. She opened the door to her house, turned on a lamp, then hobbled to a chair. After a few minutes, she went to the bathroom, wet a towel and washed her tear-stained face, and lit up a joint. "What am I gonna do now?" She wondered aloud. "My brand-new truck is ruined. Good thing I had my seatbelt on, or it would have killed me. Damn, my ankle hurts." Anne Marie continued her thought process aloud. There was no phone in the house, so she just kept setting, rubbing her face and puffing on a joint. Suddenly, a knock came on the door. Anne Marie shouted from her seated position, "Come in."

Her two friends Andy and his girlfriend, Anna, stuck their head in the door and shouted, "Anne Marie, there's a truck just like yours down at the bottom of the hill. It's really a mess."

"Well yes, I know that," Anne Marie replied. "It is my damn truck."

"It is? Geez, Anne Marie, it's really tore up. Are you okay?"

"I was until I jumped out the window and sprained my ankle. Now I can't walk. Will you guys take me back down there and see if I can figure out what to do?"

The three headed for the car parked out front. Anne Marie hobbled along on her sprained ankle. Her face was swathed in pain every time she took a step. Anna came around to help her get in the car. "Girl, I think you need to go to the hospital ER. That ankle looks bad," Ann said.

"Just lift my foot up into the car. I'll make it," Anne Marie said as she tried to climb in the backseat.

When they arrived at the bottom of the hill, they were greeted by flashing red and blue lights. The cops were there as well as an ambulance. Anne Marie pulled her aching body out of her friend's car and hobbled to the accident scene. A policeman greeted her, "Ma'am please stand back."

"That's my flipping truck in the ditch," Anne Marie answered.

"Really?" the policeman said, "Well, could I see your license and insurance card, please?"

"Here's my driver's license. I don't have the insurance card with me, but it's insured. I assure you," Anne Marie said as another tear streaked down her dusty face.

The policeman called for a wrecker, and Anne Marie realized as her truck was being lifted back on its wheels that she was lucky. Even though the truck was totaled, she had survived, and the policeman didn't even ask if she had been drinking. He just wrote her a ticket for failure to control a motor vehicle and no insurance card. She watched as the tow truck left with her wrecked pickup. The paramedics on the ambulance asked her if she would like them to look at her ankle, so Anne Marie set down on the back of the ambulance and watched as they taped it. *Geez, what a night,* Anne Marie thought. Out loud, she asked. "You guys have any pain medicine you could give me?"

Two weeks had passed since Anne Marie had totaled her pickup. She found her insurance card, and that removed the ticket for that burden. However, she still had to pay for the failure to control motor vehicle ticket. Fortunately, she did have full coverage on the wrecked pickup; so as she waited for the settlement, she got a rental car to drive. One night, someone knocked on the door; and when Anne Marie answered, it she stepped back in surprise.

Standing on the porch with a suitcase in hand was her daughter, Amelia. "Well, hello baby," Anne Marie said. "What are you doing?"

"I've come to live with you, Momma. Daddy kicked me out."

"Do what? I don't understand what you're telling me, Amelia. Your dad kicked you out?" Anne Marie stared at her daughter in disbelief. Amelia and her father had always been very close. For him to kick her out did not even compute in Anne Marie's mind.

Amelia stood shivering on Anne Marie's front porch. Uncontrolled tears started streaming down her face. "Momma, I'm pregnant," She whispered.

"Pregnant? Did you say pregnant? You're only fourteen years old, young lady. How can you be pregnant?" Anne Marie questioned with fury on her face.

"The same way you were Momma."

"Oh give me a break. I was at least sixteen."

"Well, whatever. I'm here, and I am pregnant."

"Oh, your dad's got a lot of explaining to do. Kick you out, how dare he?" Anne Marie was furious. "Where's Jacob? Is he gonna kick him out too?"

"No, Jacob is at Dad's. Dad's girlfriend watches him while Daddy's at work."

"Oh, well that's just wonderful. How convenient for her," Anne Marie retorted.

She closed the front door as Amelia came in with her suitcase. She had just finished a shot of tequila and a joint. Her head was swimming. What was she supposed to do with a fourteen-year-old pregnant child? *Damn you, Cliff. Damn you to hell and back*, she thought. Then she added, *Thanks a lot, God. You're certainly looking out for me, aren't you? I'm gonna be a grandmother before I'm thirty-two years old. Now ain't that just grand?*

Anne Marie smirked.

Out loud, she said, "Who's the father, Amelia, do you even know?"

"Yes, Mother, I know. His name is Brad," Amelia said.

"Well, call that little MF, and get his ass over here. I want to have a talk with him." Anne Marie was furious. Her face was red, and she was swearing like a sailor.

"Mother, please calm down. It's not all Brad's fault. I'm half to blame."

"Oh you, stupid girl, I know that. How old is this thug?"

"He's seventeen."

"I outa press charges on the little bastard," Anne Marie said as she paced the floor.

"Could this wait until tomorrow?" Amelia asked with choked breath.

"No, it can't wait. I want to see him right now, right this minute. Get him over here!" Anne Marie was dialing the telephone. The voice on the other end answered, and Anne Marie said, "Is that halfwit ex of mine home yet?"

"Who do you mean?" The other party asked.

"Oh, you know damn well who I mean," Anne Marie said, "while I have you on the phone, bitch, I want you to know if you ever lay a hand on either one of my kids, your ass is mine. All this time, I felt like I was the sorriest mother that ever lived, but at least my kids had a good daddy. Little did I know, the man I always worshiped and felt like he was perfect was so imperfect? What kind of daddy kicks his pregnant daughter out? Hell, he knows I'm no good, why would he send her to me?"

Annie Marie slammed the phone down as another knock sounded. She walked to the front door, eyes ablaze with anger and jerked it open.

There stood a young man visible shaken. "Who the hell are you?" Anne Marie screamed.

"Momma, that's Brad." Amelia said.

"So you're the little bastard that knocked up my daughter?" Annie Marie snapped.

The young man just stood there with his head down. "Get your ass in here right now. You and I are gonna have a heart to heart talk," Anne Marie screamed to the top of her lungs.

After that night, things calmed down for a while. Jacob, Anne Marie's son, would come over to visit on occasion, but Anne Marie always was stoned. His visits ended with her blacked out on the couch.

Amelia gave birth to a beautiful baby boy. When she came home from the hospital, she and the baby stayed in her room. Anne Marie had very little to do with Amelia or the baby. It was hard on Amelia. She was only fifteen and was having to learn how to be a mother with no example to follow. She and Anne Marie were constantly fighting and arguing about something. Finally in desperation, Amelia moved back home with her daddy.

Anne Marie was glad Amelia was out of the house. The guilt she felt every time she looked at her and the baby was annoying. *Let Cliff deal with that*, Anne Marie thought. That was always her escape. If she didn't like something, she would just pass it on to whoever was sober. The blackouts were almost daily now. Anne Marie remembered very little after nine o'clock at night.

Anne Marie got a job at O'Leary's bar. She had never been a bartender before, but it was convenient. She would drain anyone's drink if they left it setting on the bar, and if she didn't know how to mix a drink, she would just have the customer tell her how much of what went in it. She didn't care much for mixed drinks. She preferred to drink it straight up. As far as Anne Marie was concerned, it was the perfect job. She could drink all the booze, and she got paid too.

One night, a stranger came in for a drink. Anne Marie had never seen him before, and he kept flirting with her. He told her how hot she looked, and she did what she always did when a new man came into her life. She slept with him. The next morning, she awoke with a pounding head ache and the stranger beside her. "What the hell is your name?" she asked.

"Bill, just plain Bill," The stranger replied.

"Well, just plain Bill, why don't you make me a cup of coffee while I get a shower." Anne Marie laughed. "I'm sure you know where the kitchen is."

After their first night, Bill spent every waking hour at the bar where Anne Marie worked. He didn't have a job, so his spare time was used just setting at the bar and watching Anne Marie work. This got real old to her real quick. She and Bill fought all the time about something. One weekend, they went to Anne Marie's family reunion. She was sitting on the front porch, talking to her cousins that she hadn't seen in years when Bill walked by and kicked her boot. "Let's go," he stated.

"You go. I'm not ready to leave," Anne Marie said.

Bill flipped her on the back of the head with his hand. That infuriated Anne Marie. She jumped to her feet and smacked him across the face. He pushed her back, and about that time, some of Anne Marie's cousins got in on the action. The last time she saw Bill that night, he was running down the road with three of her cousins right behind him. That made Anne Marie happy, because now maybe he would leave. But he didn't. When Anne Marie got home, he was sound asleep in her bed.

He's like a bad penny, Anne Marie thought, *he just keeps showing up*. She lay down next to him and soon was fast asleep.

9

The affair with Bill ended one day when Anne Marie showed up at her friend's house in Oklahoma. Sarah was the friend's name, and she opened her door to find a blood-covered Anne Marie standing there.

"What in God's earth happened to you, Anne Marie? Come in, and let me wash some of that blood off you," Sarah said.

Anne Marie gladly followed her into the bathroom where try as she might, Sarah couldn't find where the blood was coming from. Anne Marie was hopping around on one foot and couldn't figure out why she couldn't walk on her left foot.

"See if my foot's bleeding," Anne Marie said.

"No, there's no cut place on your foot, Anne Marie, but it sure is swollen. What happened to it?"

"Damn if I know," Anne Marie replied. "It just hurts like a son of a bitch."

Anne Marie found out years later that she and Bill had got into a big fight, and he had stomped her foot to get her off of him. Her foot was broken in three places. After that episode, she moved back home with her momma. She never saw Bill again. That was fine with her. She figured that was good news, sort of like good riddance to bad garbage.

Momma had remarried, and her new husband, TJ, had a son named Tommy. Tommy had just got out of prison, and he helped Anne Marie move her things in. It didn't take long for Anne Marie to start dating Tommy. She reasoned they were no blood kin; after all, he was her step-brother. He worked putting underground cable in and made a fair amount of money. He loved the pain killer dilaudid. Anne Marie didn't care for downers, so she smoked a lot of pot while he was high on pain pills. She justified her smoking more pot with the fact she was trying to cut down on her drinking because she had started throwing up blood.

Anne Marie had got another car with the insurance settlement on her pickup, and one morning, she was taking Momma to work. It was raining, and the road was slick. A woman in a white pickup pulled out in front of Anne Marie, and she couldn't stop, she t-boned the woman's truck. Anne Marie was buckled in, so she wasn't hurt, and she had brought her dog Fancy with her that morning. Fancy was a black Labrador. The dog was barking, and Anne Marie was cussing. The bumper to her car lay in the street, and the woman's pickup wasn't hurt. Anne Marie found out the woman had no insurance, and so Anne Marie was glad she had full insurance coverage because her car was totaled.

Anne Marie didn't think she was hurt in the wreck at all. She and the dog Fancy finally made it home. Anne Marie lit up a joint, and she tried to relax. Late that afternoon, she developed a bad headache that Tommy's painkillers couldn't stop. By the next morning, she knew she had to see a doctor.

She showed up at a neurologist office in Fort Worth. He ran a cat scan on Anne Marie and discovered she had a sub-arachnoid cyst on the front of her brain the size of a dime. The neurologist said it wasn't anything to worry about. After a while, the headaches got fewer and further between. Anne Marie soon forgot there was anything wrong with her. She went back to her favorite sport—drinking and smoking pot. From the settlement she got for her wrecked car, she could afford to buy quarter pounds of pot. That way, she didn't run out as quick. She always had a beer in the fridge and pot stashed away somewhere. Anne Marie hid the balance of the cash in different places in hopes no one would find it.

Tommy took Anne Marie to New Mexico. She was excited as she had never been out of Texas except to Oklahoma. On their way, they stopped at the Cadillac ranch and made pictures on Route 66. The part Anne Marie could remember was very nice, but she remembered little because she would drink then blackout. She couldn't remember what they did or where they went. Finally, they ended up back at Momma and TJ's in a little room at the back of the house.

Anne Marie knew that Tommy liked Dilaudids but the day she caught him shooting up with them, she almost fainted. She wanted no part of needles and swore she would never do that. She found out that TJ liked them too and soon discovered that Momma also had taken up the habit. Anne Marie went to get some money she had hidden, only to discover it was gone. Tommy had found it and used $1,000 to buy dope. Most of Anne Marie's money had gone up Tommy's arm. She was furious. Finally, she remembered another hiding place and found $500 of her money Tommy had overlooked. She and Tommy got into a big fight, and he slapped her hard in front of Momma. Momma picked up whatever she could lay her hands on and punched him in the eye. Tommy and Anne Marie's relationship was over. Anne Marie was relieved she had bought a little Honda with the money she got for the settlement on the wreck. At least she had transportation. Hiding the money in different places had saved her. Except for the times she couldn't remember where she put it. But with her last $500, she moved out of Momma's house. She didn't want any more to do with Tommy. She knew he would continue to hang out at TJ and Momma's and do dope with them, so the best place for Anne Marie was away from that place.

In the weeks and months that followed Anne Marie's departure, when she did go see Momma, she would find the whole bunch stoned and nodding off to sleep, so messed up they could hardly speak. The dilaudids were expensive at $30 a pill, so TJ would go to the doctor and complain about some ache and get a prescription for more pain pills. Then he would sell part of them and shoot up the rest. When they were gone, he would start all over again. All Anne Marie knew was she wanted no part of needles. She knew nothing about addiction, and she reasoned in her mind, after all, all she did was smoke pot and stay drunk. That made her so superior to these people. Later on in Anne Marie's life, she would learn that Tommy followed the path of most drug users. He overdosed one night and killed himself.

When Anne Marie moved out from Momma's, she found a little apartment that she loved. It was located inside a huge house that had been turned into four apartments. It was the first time she had a home completely by herself. At first, it was scary, but then she discovered she liked her privacy. No one to tell her what to do, no one to check what time she got home, and no one to answer to but herself.

One night, Anne Marie, her sister Rachel, and brother Cade met at the local pool hall. Anne Marie loved to play pool, so she was excited about having a night out with her siblings. Rachel asked Anne Marie what was a good drink, and Anne Marie replied, "A Colorado bulldog." Great drink but you have to be careful; it will slip up on you.

Rachel had two bulldogs and started on her third when she became violently ill. She went running off to the bathroom, and Anne Marie chuckled to herself. "Lightweight."

After a few minutes, Cade became very concerned about Rachel and insisted Anne Marie go check on her. Begrudgingly, Anne Marie headed to the bathroom. When she opened the door, she was greeted by Rachel lying on the floor, one shoe on, one shoe off inside the bathroom stall. Her shorts were unzipped and panties and shorts half way to her knees. She had passed out in the middle of the floor. Anne Marie struggled to get Rachel to her knees then to her feet. She zipped up her shorts and headed out the door, dragging Rachel more than Rachel walking. Cade met them at the door and said he would take her home. Anne Marie thought that was a good idea and told Cade she wasn't ready to leave yet. She wanted to play some more pool. What she really wanted to do was continue to play pool with the guy she had just met named Lance.

Anne Marie continued to drink Colorado bulldogs until she blacked out. The next morning, she woke on a boat. She didn't know where she was or where her clothes were. Finally, she found her clothes and went up on deck. There stood Lance smiling at her. She found out the boat belonged to his brother. After she blacked out, he had driven her and her car to the boat where they had continued to drink and party. She really likes Lance. They got along truly well, and he never argued with her about anything. They had fun. Anne Marie found another job at another bar and soon she was bar tendering and making pretty good money. Lance had reintroduced her to speed. She had tried speed before and really liked it. Soon she was doing meth before, during, and after work to keep her going. She hardly saw her children anymore or her new grandchild. She told herself they all were better off without her. She didn't want them to see her drunk and strung out. Her life was gone down the toilet, and she didn't care. She thumbed her nose up at the world.

Anne Marie and Lance started dating regularly, and finally he moved in with her. Anne Marie worked nights, and all the neighbors worked days; so when she came home, they were leaving for work, and that made the apartment nice and quiet for her to sleep days. In truth, however, there was very little sleeping done. She was doing more and more meth. This wired her pretty high, and she would snort it until her nose started bleeding then she started smoking it on foil. She met a lot of meth heads. They were called Twickers around town. Late night, Anne Marie would hang with them before she finally went home. Twickers don't sleep much and seldom eat. She lost weight very quickly, going from a size sixteen to a size three in two months. She finally was skinny again, and she loved it. Her boss at work and Lance taught her to play chess. She got pretty good at it. She played while she was at work until it got too busy then she would play when she got home. That was the only time Anne Marie was able to sit still.

Lance worked delivering furniture and was gone a lot, but things were still very good between he and Anne Marie, until she slept with a guy named Sam.

Sam had a nice truck, his own house, and owned a car business. Anne Marie and Lance soon parted ways. Lance left her, and Anne Marie couldn't blame him. She would have done the same. She was like a tornado, ripping through people's lives and leaving nothing but debris in the wake. She would do terrible things and never once think of the consequences. The relationship between Sam and her didn't last long. He was arrogant, jealous, and possessive, and she hated that.

One day, a guy came in the bar who claimed to be with Music Scene Magazine. He kept asking Anne Marie to take her picture. He kept telling her he was a model photographer.

"Then why in hell do you want to make my picture?" Anne Marie asked "I'm not model material."

"Oh, yes you are. You're smoking hot," He said. He went on to explain that he took pictures for a living, and models paid him good money to do just that.

"Well, I sure as hell am not paying you anything," Anne Marie stated.

He wanted to come to her place and make her picture. Anne Marie didn't trust him as far as she could throw him, so she asked one of her friends to come over while he made pictures.

The photo session went well enough, and in a few days, the photographer brought the pictures into the bar for Anne Marie to see. However, Anne Marie's modeling career ended when the photographer wanted to send the picture to the Easy Rider magazine. Anne Marie didn't want her picture in a magazine. The pictures were passed around for all to see. Finally, she found the pictures with a guy named Roy. He had been coming in the bar for at least two months, hitting on her. At the time, she was with Lance, and Roy would set next to him and hit on Anne Marie. Lance never got mad; he just laughed.

After Anne Marie's breakup with Lance, her life went from bad to worse. She would wake up next to men she didn't know, in places she couldn't remember. The situations were dangerous, and only by the grace of God did someone not kill her. But she had no intention of slowing down. On her thirty-fifth birthday, a guy she did remember invited her to New Orleans to celebrate her birthday. He gave her a stuffed toy that looked like a big gorilla, and it sang "Wild Thing." They went to Bourbon Street and set in a bar drinking Bloody Marys. Anne Marie really liked them, and they had a green bean in them to stir the drink. She found out later that the green bean had been soaked in Everclear. The drinks hit her hard, and she wound up giving her pants to the parking garage attendant as a tip. She blacked out and her date took her back to her motel room. Her key was lost, and the guy ended up taking the window air conditioner out and crawling in the room so he could open the door and get her inside. The next morning, the guy was still angry at the whole situation, and he and Anne Marie got in a big argument. She told him to " F——ck " off and came home. That was the last time she saw him.

Roy kept hanging around the bar where Anne Marie worked. He kept asking her out, and she kept saying no. Finally one night, she agreed to go out with him. At the time, Anne Marie was doing a lot of meth. He had never tried it; he liked cocaine and crack. Anne Marie had tried coke before, and she liked it; but it was too expensive, so she gave it up. She didn't even know what crack looked like. She hadn't tried it, so the two exchanged their preferences. The two smoked some meth and coke. She didn't know she could smoke coke. She decided she didn't like the coke as much as she did the meth. After their party, Roy came home with Anne Marie. He told her he owned a house trailer, and his mom lived there with him. What he didn't tell Anne Marie was that he also had a girlfriend who had a child that lived there as well, and they had talked of marriage.

Roy went home the next morning, but that evening late, he returned with some clothes. He had been there a couple of days when Anne Marie found out about the girlfriend. Roy refused to go home, so the girlfriend moved out. Roy would borrow Anne Marie's car for fifteen minutes and return three hours later. He fixed Anne Marie's car radio and hooked it up to speakers. Then the headlights didn't work. Anne Marie gave him hell most all the time about one thing or another, yet they still had a good time together. Another friend named Cecil moved in with them too. The trio shared the same apartment. Roy and Anne Marie became a twosome, and Cecil continued to live there for a while.

Roy worked for a big trucking company. He was good-looking, tall, dark, and the preverbal handsome. He was half Filipino and had dark skin and green eyes. Anne Marie fell in love.

The fact that Roy was six years her junior made no difference. Roy took her out to meet his mom, and Anne Marie found out it was his mom's trailer Roy had been living in, and he had been driving her truck. After their visit, Roy decided he was going back on the road and drive the big rigs. He asked Anne Marie to come with him. She mused it over in her mind and thought, *What the heck. I can travel and see the country.* So she said yes. What she didn't know was her drinking and drug using had to cease while she was in the truck. That came as a big shock and almost caused her to back out going with Roy. She couldn't even do pot because if DOT caught Roy, he would lose his CDL driver's license. So Anne Marie went cold turkey. That's how much she loved Roy. She wanted to be with him more than she wanted the drugs. Of course at times, they would find a bar and have a few drinks. And of course, as were most things in Anne Marie's life, her being off drugs was short lived.

One night, after the big eighteen-wheeler was safely parked, Roy asked Anne Marie if she wanted to smoke some crack. She had never smoked any, so of course, she said she would like to try it. She didn't know how to light it up; she thought you smoked it in foil like you did meth. Roy showed her exactly how it was done, and she was off on another high. But Anne Marie didn't like the way it made her feel. She just wanted more and more, and she hated what it did to Roy. He would see imaginary things. One night, he peeped out the curtains of the sleeping cab and saw a little Mexican setting on the fender of the truck. The Mexican had on a sombrero, and Roy was afraid of him. Roy would open and shut the curtains, turn out the lights, and tell Anne Marie to get down so he couldn't see them. Anne Marie looked and saw nothing. She realized Roy was hallucinating from the crack. She told him to shut up, and then she took another puff of the crack.

Many times when they were high on crack, they would talk about Anne Marie having sex with someone and Roy watching. They thought that was funny, and the conversations involving sex were always perverted. Anne Marie didn't mind because that's all it was to her—sex and nothing more. She had been with so many men by now she had lost count, and it really didn't matter anymore. Sex was a tool to her, and she used it to get what she wanted. She felt dead inside. She hated what she saw in the mirror.

Anne Marie and Roy had many adventures on the road. They were stranded twice in Montana, visited many strip clubs and bars. Anne Marie enjoyed the strip joints more than Roy did. But despite the words of encouragement from bystanders, she never did dance in one of them. She drew the line there even though her saying was she would try anything once and more if she liked it. She never thought of the consequences or what might happen to her. Finally, she announced she'd had enough of the road, and she was ready to go home. She was ready to get back to Texas where she could at least get a shower daily, and then there was always the drugs and alcohol that were a little more available when you knew where to get them.

Anne Marie had lost the apartment when she went on the road with Roy for failure to pay the rent. That left only one place to go, and that was back to Momma's house. She moved box after box into the backroom of Momma's, and the rest of the furniture she sold.

One night, Roy showed up with a girl that he introduced as his sister. She told them that Roy's brother really wanted him to move back to Illinois and try to start his life over. He wanted what was best for Roy and encouraged him and Anne Marie to come up, and he would help Roy find a good job. Roy wouldn't consider it unless Anne Marie agreed to go with him.

Anne Marie and Roy decided to accept his brother's kind offer and once again packed what they had and headed out for Illinois. When they arrived, they were greeted by Roy's brother and sister-in-law and made welcome to their home. Anne Marie soon met all of Roy's lifelong friends and all his kinfolk. One night, some friends were over to play poker. Anne Marie had been drinking beer all day, so she was primed for anything. She and Roy got into a big argument because he wanted to go to the basement and watch a movie, and she wanted to stay upstairs and drink beer with all the new friends. Roy swung at Anne Marie but hit his sister-in-law by mistake. The cops came, and Roy was arrested for domestic abuse.

Anne Marie had no idea how she was going to get Roy out of jail. She had no money and no job. Finally, his brother took out a loan and got Roy out of jail. This was not Roy's first time in prison. When he was younger, he had been in one of Illinois prisons for two years. But when Roy got out of jail, they decided they would go visit one of Roy's friends in a different town. On the way there, the old van they were driving broke down. So typical reactions of Anne Marie and Roy, they left the van there. Now they were broke—no transportation, and no one they could go too to ask for help.

Anne Marie walked boldly up to the church door office. She went in and told her sad story to the pastor of the church. She told them they were broke down and had no food and no way to get home. The church agreed to pay for a motel room for a couple of days, and this gave Anne Marie time to go to the welfare office and beg them to help. They did give them a week of lodging and some food. One of Roy's friends named Reed had a cute little apartment—all nice and clean. And he offered to let Roy and Anne Marie stay there until they could decide what they were going to do. Reed worked at a tire shop and shared his home and food with them. He loaned Anne Marie a bike to ride. She had never been without a place to stay before, so she was very thankful to have found a Good Samaritan to help them out.

The only problem with the bike, it was December and extremely cold. She would shudder as she rode down the snow-covered streets and dreamed of Texas. She decided she would see if she could find a job as a bartender. Her newfound friend, Reed, took her shopping and bought her new clothes from the skin out. She felt very pretty when she walked in the bar to apply for a job, compliments of a Good Samaritan. She was getting homesick again, but she knew a bicycle wasn't going to get her to Texas.

Roy had seen a beat-up old truck parked in a pasture. He went to the house and knocked on the door. When a woman appeared, he asked her about the truck. She told him it had belonged to her late husband, and that it had been setting in the pasture for years. She added it didn't run, but if he could get it going, then she would give him the truck. That's all Roy wanted to hear. He got one of his new friends to help him move the car to a vacant lot that had a covered garage. He started to work on the old truck with high hopes.

Anne Marie's first night on the job as a bartender didn't start so well. She had to wear heels, and by the time she rode the bicycle to work, her feet were already killing her. The thought of wearing tennis shoes and changing once she got there never crossed her mind. But somehow, she made it through the night and then got home. She was very disappointed. She was used to making very good tips, but this first night, she only made enough to buy a pack of cigarettes. She decided life sucked.

While Anne Marie slept during the day, Roy worked on the old truck. Finally, the beat-up, rusted truck roared to life. Roy was so proud of himself as was Anne Marie. Finally, they had wheels once again. On New Year's Day of 2001, she called home to wish her sister happy birthday. Rachel told her that TJ, Anne Marie's step dad, had died on the Christmas Eve of 2000. "My God," Anne Marie said, "has it really been that long since I called home?"

"I'm afraid so," Rachel replied, "I'm afraid so."

Anne Marie's cousin got them a job offer in Arizona. It was a big company and always in need of construction workers. So Anne Marie and Roy were off to start another journey. Roy asked Anne Marie to marry him. One day, they took off work and went to the justice of the peace and got married. They found a room in a old motel that rented rooms by the day or the week. The construction company hired Roy as a pipefitter, and Anne Marie was hired as a pipefitter's helper. Roy made $18 an hour, and Anne Marie made $14. They worked twelve to fourteen hours a day, seven days a week. It wasn't long until they were high rolling once again.

Roy and Anne Marie found an old Airstream travel trailer. They bought it for $1,000. It looked like a big beer can. Anne Marie said, "All it needs is flowers painted on the side and a peace sign." But it was home. The owner of the motel let them park their trailer on the back lot, along with their beat-up old pickup truck.

One morning, their old truck wouldn't start. Roy got a guy to help him get it started, and then he told Anne Marie after work he would take the truck and see if he could get it fixed. Anne Marie got in from work that afternoon and saw that Roy wasn't home, and she assumed he was getting the truck fixed. It was past 10 p.m., and still Roy wasn't home. Anne Marie walked the floor all night long, waiting and looking for Roy. The next day, she didn't go to work; she planned on spending the day looking for Roy. About eight that morning, Roy came walking up to the trailer. He was walking; no truck in sight. Anne Marie flew into him like a bantam rooster, "Where the hell have you been all night, and where's our truck?" She screamed.

"It's buried out in the desert up to the door windows in mud," Roy said.

"You liar," Anne Marie said. "How can anything be buried in mud in the desert?"

Roy started explaining to Anne Marie. "I went by the bank and got $500 then I bought some crack. I was going to ride around and smoke up the crack, but I got lost on some back roads. I drove through a mud puddle that I didn't know was there, and the pickup got stuck. I tried to get it out until I ran out of gas."

"Liar, liar, you are such a liar. There are no mud puddles in the middle of the desert. What kind of idiot do you think I am?" Anne Marie shouted to the top of her lungs.

Roy went on to explain that he tried to walk home, but every time he got out of the truck and started walking, the coyotes would start yelping and scaring him. He also explained the bad part was he ran out of a light and couldn't even smoke the crack. Anne Marie didn't believe a word he was saying until he opened his hand and showed her all the crack he had left. They sit down and started smoking the crack so she could calm down, then they went to look for the truck. Sure enough, the truck was buried up to the windows in a mud hole. She just stood there and shook her head as Roy and a friend from work pulled the truck out. It was out of gas, so they had brought a two-gallon container of gasoline. Soon the old truck roared to life once again, and Roy and Anne Marie had wheels.

Their boss at work also lived in the motel where their trailer was parked. He started questioning Anne Marie at work about what they were doing. She immediately told him he wasn't her daddy, and whatever they were doing was none of his business. Then she asked for a transfer to another department. Anne Marie and Roy decided they would move their trailer to a trailer park down the street so their boss and his wife wouldn't know their business quite as easy.

Anne Marie and Roy were working lots of long hours. She decided that if she got some meth, it would give her a much-needed boost. No one around there had any meth, but she met two guys at work who told her they had something better than meth. Curious, Anne Marie asked them what could be better than meth. They called it Glass or Ice. To Anne Marie, it looked like broken shards of glass, and it was twice as strong as meth. She fell in love with it from the first time she tried it. She tried snorting it first, but it caused her to have severe nose bleeds, and it burned like fire in her nose and made her feel as though her head would explode. So she learned how to smoke it, and then she learned how to make her own glass pipes. Before long, she smoked as much as she could, as often as she could. Her pot smoking and drinking decreased immensely, because now she stayed high on glass.

One day, the department she had transferred to moved her back to her former job. Her old boss threw a fit and said he didn't want her anywhere around him. When the supervisors told him she was going to stay there, he got mad and quit. Well that was fine with Anne Marie; she was glad he was gone. But in the weeks that followed, the power plant they were working on in Casa Grande, Arizona was drawing to an end. The company started laying people off. Roy was one of the first ones to go. Anne Marie went to her immediate boss and told him she had to keep her job since Roy had been laid off. After all, her income was the only income they had now. The boss liked her and agreed to keep her on as long as he could. One morning, they announced there was going to be a random drug test. Anne Marie's name was drawn. She went to her boss, thanked him for his kindness to her, and then she quit. She knew she couldn't pass the drug test.

Roy and Anne Marie were okay for a while. They had made enough to keep the rent paid to park their trailer, but eventually, Anne Marie was smoking up what money they had saved. Roy and Anne Marie fought all the time unless they were high. Soon all their money was spent on glass. Now they were broke and had no job. Anne Marie had lived for months on Mountain Dew and Snickers. Soon a size three was too big for her. One night, Roy slipped a jewelry make up box Anne Mare had hung on to, out of the trailer. He hid it in a little shack he had built behind the trailer. When Anne Marie discovered it was gone, she was furious. It contained all the worldly treasures she had. In it was her Poppa's knife and several other things she treasured. She went all over the trailer park, asking if anyone had seen her little jewelry box. No one had and she burst into tears. All the worldly possessions had gone away and left her with nothing but a hangover and a broken heart.

Anne Marie found out that Roy had quit smoking ice and started shooting up dope. She was so angry with him until he talked her into trying it. She couldn't muster the nerve to stick the needle in her arm, so she had Roy do it for her. The first time she shot up, she loved it. It was an instant high, and from then on, that's the only way Anne Marie would do dope. Before long, Anne Marie was doing things she had sworn she would never do. She had lost all morals and all values. All she worried about was her next high. She would do anything to get her next high. She would lie, cheat, or steal. At one time in her life, she had believed that what went around came around, and she was reaping her repayment big time.

One day, Roy and Anne Marie met a businessman who needed help moving some things from Colorado to Arizona. Roy and Anne Marie needed money, so they volunteered to help with the move. On the way back to Arizona, they had the radio on and heard about the 9-11 Twin Towers incident in New York. This scared Anne Marie to death, all she could think about was, *What if Jesus comes back to earth and finds me? This could be the "end," and I'm lost and far away from God.*

The feeling that her life was spinning out of control didn't last long for Anne Marie. As soon as she and Roy got back to Arizona and collected their money for helping move the office equipment from Colorado, they were off to the dope house. As long as she was high, Anne Marie didn't have to deal with guilty feelings. It did, however, make her homesickness more pronounced. She started in on Roy to get her back to Texas. Her being strung out and homeless on the streets of a city in Arizona would have scared a sober man.

Roy's ingenious way of hustling produced a beat-up old car. Anne Marie stole some stuff from the people who had been kind enough to try and help her. She pawned the things, and soon they had enough money to fill the old cars gas tank and head east toward Texas. It didn't take long until they were broke again, so they stopped at a truck stop to beg for money. They spent the night in the truck stop's parking lot, and the next day, a stranger gave them ten dollars for gas. Anne Marie looked for a church, and when she found one, she went inside to tell her sad story to the pastor. The church gave them a voucher for gas. Once the gas tank on the old car was filled, they were on the road again Texas bound.

The flashing red lights behind them pulled Anne Marie up short. By this time in her life, she had a relationship with the law that was less than savory. As the cop walked up to the driver's window, Anne Marie tried to slip down farther in the passenger seat. She looked at the policeman in contempt as he asked for license and registration. Of course, they had neither; and when the license plate was run, the policeman got the owner's name and found out that he wanted the car back. He didn't report it stolen, merely claimed the car.

Anne Marie watched as the tow truck hauled her hope for Texas away. This time, however, Anne Marie had a new experience with the police. This time, they paid for their room. Taking advantage of their newfound luck, they showered and cleaned up and tried to figure out how to finish their journey. Anne Marie thumbed through her tattered old address book and tried to find someone's name that might help them. She came across her Aunt B's phone number. She hadn't spoken to her aunt in years, but before long, Anne Marie found herself dialing her aunt's number collect. Explaining her sad story, she touched her aunt's heart. Aunt B sent them two Greyhound bus tickets for Texas. Anne Marie leaned her head back against the bus seat and closed her eyes. Perhaps she would sleep all the way home.

10

When Anne Marie and Roy arrived in Texas, they went straight to Momma's house. That seemed to be the place Anne Marie landed every time. She promised Momma she and Roy would stay in the back of the house and not bother anyone. Of course, her promises meant nothing; and before long, Anne Marie and Roy realized no one around here even knew what "ice" was. Anne Marie's drug of choice couldn't be found, so she was back on meth. It never occurred to her that while she was sober, maybe she should just stay that way. No, meth was readily available, and she was always a willing participant.

On March 16, 2002, Anne Marie came home to an empty house. High as usual, she went next door to inquire of the neighbor if she knew where Momma was. To her surprise, the neighbor informed her that Momma was at the hospital. She was in shock. What was wrong? The neighbor explained that it wasn't Momma that was sick, but her sister Maddie.

Anne Marie rushed to the hospital to be met by her brother and Momma. To her surprise, they informed her that Maddie was dead. "This can't be happening," Anne Marie screamed. Maddie had everything. She had a beautiful family, a loving husband, and a registered nursing degree. How could Maddie be dead? She had gone to the hospital with an earache. No one dies from an earache.

Later, Anne Marie found out that Maddie had TTP, Thrombotic Thrombocytopenic Purpura. It was a rare blood disease. Maddie didn't even know she had it, and suddenly, she was dead.

Anne Marie had even more reason to stay high and be mad at God. One more time, he had taken a person that she loved with all her heart. Once more, he had ripped her heart out of her chest. Maddie was the best person she had ever known. Once more, she raised her fist toward the heavens and cursed God. The last thing she recalled was a conversation she had had with Maddie. Maddie had begged her to please get her life straight. She had pleaded and tried to reason with Anne Marie about the way she was living her life.

Yeah and look what you got, Maddie. You got death, Anne Marie thought.

Roy had found a dope connection across the river on the Oklahoma side. Roy did odd jobs for the man in exchange for dope. One day, he and Anne Marie were there when the sheriff's department showed up looking for the owner. Anne Marie freaked out. She feared she would go to jail in Oklahoma, and she did not want that. The cops, however, were pretty laid-back about the whole thing. They just took their names and addresses and searched Anne Marie's purse. Fortunately, they found nothing because Anne Marie had her pipe in her back pocket.

After that, she never went back with Roy. She would stay home and let him go score for her. If he didn't return quickly enough, she would get fighting mad at him. But as soon as she got high, she would mellow out and be all right.

Roy started hanging out with a guy called Outlaw, and he had this stuff called red. But it didn't look like the "red" Anne Marie was used to. Doing meth was getting too expensive, and so Roy and Anne Marie started finding other ways to get it. The two decided they would do their own cooking of red in the backroom of Momma's house. Roy and Anne Marie were novices to the cooking process, but they located a man who knew all about it. They hustled all the things needed to cook off a batch. To their disgust, it had a horrible smell. Anne Marie worried the entire time that it cooked for fear someone would smell it and call the cops.

One night, they cooked off a batch, and it didn't turn out. Outlaw said it was locked. Anne Marie had no idea what "locked" meant. She just knew there would be no dope tonight. Several people came and tried to unlock it all to no avail. The next night, Roy was outside, and the police showed up. They arrested Roy for some unpaid tickets he had. Anne Marie was scared to death.

If they came in the house, they would find the lab set up, and everyone there would be arrested including Momma for allowing this to go on in her house. Anne Marie had promised Momma some of the dope when it was cooked off, but there would be none of that this night. That's when Anne Marie started liking anhydrous ammonia. Anhydrous always turned out, so she didn't know what all went in to making it, but figured she could find out and cook her own.

Roy set the ticket fines out in jail, and he was out in a few days. Anne Marie, Roy, and Outlaw went to a farm house and stole some anhydrous. Most farmers kept the fertilizer on hand, so finding it was generally pretty easy. They went to the river to cook it off. It was a lot faster than red, and smelled a lot worse. Fortunately down by the river, no one could smell it, and they were safe from prying eyes. This became a new way of life for Anne Marie; she was always looking over her shoulder now for the cops. She was lying, cheating, stealing, hustling, just to get her next bump. Most of the time, she was so skitzed out she wasn't even aware of her surroundings.

Roy got tired of doing all the leg work for Outlaw and not getting much dope in return. He and Anne Marie decided they would do their own cooking and keep the dope themselves. They had friends who allowed them to use their house. One day, Anne Marie pulled up and got out of the truck. As she stepped upon the porch, she heard a loud explosion. Her hair blew back, and she could see flames. The metal shelf on the side of the porch was blown down, and all the plants spilled out on the floor. Anne Marie realized the entire house was on fire. She ran screaming to the front yard. In a few minutes, Roy came running out of the house. They huddled together by the car, and then Anne Marie screamed, "Let's get the hell outta here, Roy. The cops will be here any minute." They hurried away just as the cops and fire department pulled in. Anne Marie found out later that the owner of the house had been burned very badly. They were lucky to have escaped with their life.

The cops started showing up on a consistent base at Momma's house. They were always looking for Roy. Of course, Roy was seldom there. He was always out hustling for drugs. One day, one of the cops told Anne Marie if she didn't get away from Roy, she was going to wind up in jail just like him. Those words would come back to haunt Anne

Marie later on, but on this particular day, she defended Roy and was quick to tell the policeman that she was "in love with Roy," and he was her husband. The truth was she was in love with the dope that he provided for her.

Since Anne Marie had no vehicle to drive, she borrowed her daughter's one day to go get anhydrous. She was ready for a fix, and Roy was nowhere around, so she reasoned she would, just do it herself. She never once thought of the smell it would leave behind in the trunk of the car or how harmful it was for her daughter, son-in-law, and grandson to inhale the fumes. And of course, she neglected to tell them the car would smell horrible for days to come because of the anhydrous.

They met a new guy who had wheels and an apartment, so Anne Marie and Roy moved right in with him. There were woods behind the apartment, and that made cooking the dope a lot easier. They could hide in the woods, and no one would be the wiser of what was going on. Anne Marie didn't go to the cook offs, but she would help make the preparations. She loved to powder the anhydrous and watch it snow. The more snow, the more dope, and that was all Anne Marie lived for.

There was a trailer on Main Street where a lot of the dope cookers would hang out. Anne Marie started frequenting the place until one day, she noticed two pickup trucks seemed to always be parked close to the house. Her paranoia warned her that the police were watching the comings and goings of everyone who went to that place. Anne Marie tried to figure a way that she could go to the trailer without being seen. She was doing bump after bump. Each time she did one, it would drop her to her knees and inside she was screaming, *God, help me.* She knew she was getting so far out and so out of touch with reality that someday she couldn't come back.

There were days that Anne Marie neither ate nor slept. The days turned into weeks. One instance she was up for fourteen days. She started hearing things and seeing things that weren't there. She saw shadows that no one else could see and heard voices that no one else heard. She thought the voices were talking to her, yet she couldn't understand what they were saying. Then she thought she had bugs under her skin, and she would set and pick at the bugs, trying to get them out making big sores on her face and body. She would explain the sores as pimples, but in her mind, she knew insanity lurked just around the corner for her. She could call the sores pimples, but she couldn't explain away the track marks up and down her arms. She didn't even try to hide them anymore. She had become a junkie—something she had sworn would never happen to her. She was living the life of a skitzer. When she looked in the mirror, she hardly recognized the person she saw. She hated herself for what she had become. Inside she was screaming for help, but she couldn't break free from the hold the dope had on her.

One day, the DEA showed up at the apartment. Anne Marie let them in. What choice did she have? They asked permission to search the place, and she let them. She didn't care at this point; she was just tired and worn out. They found two pages of evidence to prove that she and Roy were cooking and selling meth. They really were after Roy, but since Anne Marie was there, they told her if she cooperated it would go better for her. They ask her to call Roy and let them talk to him. She did as they requested. When Roy got on the phone, they told him if he didn't come home and give himself up, they would charge Anne Marie with all the crimes.

Roy returned to the apartment and told the DEA all the stuff was his. They agreed not to charge Anne Marie with the evidence they had found but did arrest Roy and her— Anne Marie for the marijuana they found in her purse. They took both of them to jail. One of their friends bonded Anne Marie out, but Roy wasn't so lucky.

Anne Marie tried to get the money to bond Roy out of jail, but everyone she knew turned her down. Finally, a girl she had met at the trailer told her if she could gather up enough stuff, she could sell it. Anne Marie gathered up all the things that people had brought to them to pay for the dope they sold. Most of the things were stolen, but Anne Marie was desperate. After all, Roy had sacrificed himself for her. At least, that's how she reasoned the events that had taken place. Anne Marie loaded up the girls van with TVs, stereos, tools, and a bunch of other stuff. The girl left to go sell it.

Hours passed, and the girl with everything Anne Marie possessed did not return. Anne Marie waited, and with each passing hour, she grew angrier. Finally, Anne Marie left to look for her. She found her a week later, and the story the girl told was when she arrived at the fence to sell the stuff, he kept it all and refused to pay for it. What was Anne Marie to do? She certainly couldn't call the cops and report the stolen stuff she had as stolen. She grew desperate. Roy was the one who always got the dope for her. He was in jail, and she was alone. She needed a fix badly.

In jail, Roy had met a guy who talked his girlfriend into putting up the $2,000 to bail Roy out. Roy promised to pay her back just as soon as he could. Of course, he never did.

After two weeks of freedom, he and Anne Marie were right back to their old habits. In no time at all, it was business as usual for them.

One morning, Roy told Anne Marie he was going to go work on an old car he had talked someone in to giving him. She walked with him out on the patio and kissed him good-bye. All of a sudden, this premonition came over her that they needed to get out of town. She told Roy how she felt, and he just laughed at her and said, "Go get a bump. you'll feel better."

He left, and Anne Marie went about getting dressed. Her plans were to clean the apartment. Suddenly, there was a knock on the door. When she peeked through the peephole, all she could see were red flashing lights. The DEA yelled, "police." The next thing Anne Marie knew, they kicked in the door, and she was surrounded with guns pointing straight at her. She found out they arrested Roy as soon as he had left the apartment. They had been watching when they kissed good-bye and the minute he got in the parking lot they were on the scene. They arrested Anne Marie, and this time, there was no one to bond her out. She was going to be in jail for a very long time.

When they put Anne Marie in general population, she nearly freaked out. She had never been there before ,and the people who surrounded her were scary. Some were insane, waiting for transportation to an insane asylum. There were thieves, murderers, abusers, dopers, and the list was endless. She was right in the middle of them all. To make bad matters worse, she was coming down from her high. She detoxed in a jail cell, and the pain was terrible. She was shocked at how many inmates were in the "pod" she was assigned too. Twenty-four females shared a very small area.

Anne Marie didn't start any fights, but she made up her mind she wasn't taking any crap either. Most inmates left her alone, and she returned the favor. Most of them were there for meth-related charges. *I've got to get out of here*, was the only thought Anne Marie had. Immediately, she started applying for the role of "trustee." The main reason she wanted that was because she thought she might be able to hear something about Roy. Each time she applied, she was turned down, but Anne Marie kept on applying. By now she was sober and very frightened. Her family was happy she was in jail. Not for the punishment but because at least now, they knew where she was. They were glad she was there and not dead somewhere on the side of the road.

She would attend any and all Bible classes that were offered just to get out of the "pod," for a little while. Anne Marie felt she was way too far gone for God to even hear her prayers. After all, she had prayed many times for him to save her, and her present circumstance proved to her that he certainly didn't hear a word she had prayed. Attending the Bible classes gave her was just an excuse to escape that nasty small cell she shared with twenty-three other females. She hated this place.

11

One day while in a Bible class, it dawned on Anne Marie that she needed to be careful what she prayed for because she just might get it. God had heard her prayers and answered them. He just hadn't answered in the way Anne Marie had thought he would. After all, being in jail had probably saved her life. The road she had been walking was leading straight to an overdose that would take her life. Here she was, at least safe. She realized God had kept his arms around her during the worst times of her life. Then she started reading her Bible and going to church, not just to get out of the pod, but because she truthfully wanted to change her life. She wanted to once again have a relationship with Jesus Christ. God was moving in Anne Marie's life.

On one of the long days that followed her incarceration, Anne Marie was served with her indictment papers. The state of Texas was charging her with four felony indictments. They were, possession of a controlled substance, possession with intent to deliver, manufacturing a controlled substance, and attempted manufacturing. She was guilty of all except one. She didn't intend to deliver anything; she was intending to use it all herself.

Anne Marie's heart sank as she read the indictments. The realization she was probably going to be in jail for a very long time, began to sink in to her head. As she sat quietly, tears started rolling down her cheeks. One of her cell mates approached her and offered some comfort. She told Anne Marie to trace her hand on a piece of paper, and then to write on each finger and her palm, the things she wanted from God. Later, she realized God had indeed answered each of her requests. He just answered in a way she never expected.

A court-appointed attorney was assigned to Anne Marie's case. When the one time she came to talk with Anne Marie, Anne Marie told her about the indictments. She did nothing as far as Anne Marie could tell, and so Anne Marie started screaming she wanted another attorney. That wasn't going to happen, and much to Anne Marie's disgust, the woman remained her lawyer.

Fifty eight days after being placed in jail, Anne Marie made trustee. She was so excited to get out of the pod and to get two mattresses and ice for her tea. She felt a certain pride and sense of accomplishment. She started immediately to try and hear from Roy. The system put Anne Marie to work washing cars. One day, an old acquaintance came to get his car washed. Anne Marie almost hugged his neck; she was so glad to see someone she knew outside of the jail cell.

He told her that someone in Oklahoma was using her identity and writing hot checks. Anne Marie laughed and said, "You can see it ain't me. I've been in here for nearly four months now. But I know who it is." The couple she had lived with in Oklahoma had found her lost cigarette case that had her ID in it. They stole it and were using her ID to forge the checks. Silently, Anne Marie thought, *Payback is hell.* They were doing to her exactly what she had done to so many others.

Anne Marie was baptized in a big horse trough the preacher brought to the jail. After that, Anne Marie's job changed from car washer to trash picker. Anne Marie had learned she could make the most of bad situations. She loved picking up the trash because it allowed her to be outside in the sunshine and fresh air and to get some exercise. One day, they called her inside to tell her she was going to court that very day. This came as a big surprise to her. She certainly wasn't prepared for that. The last time she had been to court, one of the DA's assistants had shown up and told the court Anne Marie was a threat to society and shouldn't have her bond lowered. She wondered if today would be a repeat.

When Anne Marie arrived in court, her attorney was there waiting on her. *Big shock, she had finally done her job,* Anne Marie thought. As Anne Marie stood before the judge, she could hardly believe her ears. They offered her eight years of probation. Of course she took it, and that very day, Anne Marie went home. It had been hot summer when she went to jail, and today the north wind was blowing, and the temperature was 32 degrees. Anne Marie stood outside the jail and took a deep breath of the cold air and thanked God she was free. She didn't wait around for fear the judge would change his mind. She didn't call anyone to come and get her; she just started walking, and the cold wind bit at her thinly clad body. The only clothes she had outside of the jail uniform were thin, but she didn't care she was so happy to be free.

Anne Marie started walking to Momma's house. A pickup truck sped by her, and then the driver threw on the breaks and backed up. He asked if she wanted a ride, and Anne Marie gladly accepted. She was freezing. The Good Samaritan listened as Anne Marie told about her stay in jail and how she was just trying to get home. The driver took her all the way to Momma's house then wished her luck as she got out of the truck. When she walked in the front door, Momma and two old friends were shocked to see her. The three were already high, and it didn't take long for old habits to return to Anne Marie. Self-pity entered her as she looked around her old room and realized she had nothing left. All her stuff was gone. She tried to remember she was just happy to be out of jail.

The next day after her release from jail, Anne Marie had to report to her probation officer. She wasn't familiar with how probation worked. When she showed up, she was told her probation officer was an elderly lady named Nell. At first, she thought she could manipulate her easily. She soon found out Nell might be elderly, but she was sharp as a tack, and there would be no manipulation of her. Nell explained to her how probation was going to work. She was to pay for classes on Life Skills and go to AA meetings. Nell might as well have asked her to pay a million dollars. Anne Marie had no wheels, no money, or even the prospect for a job. All she had was a bed and a roof over her head at Momma's, and that was fading fast as no one that lived there had a job either. The bills were going unpaid, and soon all of them would be living on the street. Anne Marie decided she could care less and started going with one of her old friends to steal meat and sell to have money to buy alcohol. She didn't bother to report to her probation officer either. Anne Marie had a lot to learn about probation.

One day as they were out trying to sell the stolen meat, Anne Marie was able to get enough money to buy some alcohol. She drank the entire bottle and passed out in the backseat of her friend's car. Suddenly, red lights appeared behind them. An Oklahoma Highway Patrol officer walked up to the driver's side of the car and asked for license and registration. Not a person in the car had a driver's license. The officer confiscated the car, and all the occupants were without transportation. Walking back to Texas seemed like a reasonable thing to do at the time. The friends helped Anne Marie as she staggered down the road toward home. Later Anne Marie was to realize she had been fortunate. She wasn't supposed to even be out of the county much less in another state since she was on probation.

The third month, Anne Marie was to report to her probation officer when she decided she just wouldn't go. She didn't have the money to pay for the classes or the fines, so she would just skip going. Besides, Outlaw had called and wanted to come over, and so Anne Marie told him it would be fine. She knew she could score with him, and he would be good for at least a bump or two. Outlaw knew that Roy was in jail, and he started coming over to see Anne Marie often, always bringing her a bump. One day, Anne Marie consented to go to a motel with him. The sex she didn't want, but she sure wanted the dope Outlaw supplied. After that, Outlaw started acting like she was his girlfriend. Anne Marie hated that and told him she was married to Roy, and she was waiting for him to get out of jail so they could be together again. He ignored her, and one day, he brought her a bump he had made himself. He took one out of a bag and handed another one to Anne Marie from a different bag. Anne Marie didn't care which bag it came out of; she just wanted the dope. Outlaw did his bump and left. When Anne Marie did hers, it felt like the top of her head was coming off, and it felt like she was on fire from her head to her toes. Anne Marie knew immediately something wasn't right. There was nothing she could do about it, because it was already in her bloodstream. She became violently ill.

The next morning when Anne Marie awoke, she looked at the jeans she had on. There were holes all up and down the legs where she had wiped the dope from the blade after getting her fix. She shook her head and went into the bathroom to throw up again. She figured Outlaw had used too many batteries when he did his cooking, and that's was why her jeans had holes in them. He had a habit of always using more batteries than what was needed when he cooked off a batch. The next four days, Anne Marie drifted between consciousness and unconsciousness. She would get up and drink whiskey and then go back to bed. All the lights, water, and gas had been turned off at Momma's because no one paid the bill. On the fifth day, Anne Marie got out of bed, got dressed, and left the house full of addicts and drunks. She walked to an old friend's house and begged her to let her stay there until she felt better. Her old friend consented but with one exception—there would be no dope brought into her house. Anne Marie agreed. She had no choice; she was nearly dead. Her room had a concrete floor, a half bed, a small heater, and no carpet,. She didn't care because the room was warm. Her friend lectured her daily about the dope she was doing, but she just let it go in one ear and out the other.

Roy had received two years state time and eight years at TDC. Anne Marie knew he was going to be gone a long, long time, so she had to make plans to take care of herself.

Anne Marie's friend got her a job helping remodel an old building in town. Anne Marie didn't really care what she was doing as long as it made her a little money. She was drinking beer daily but only smoking pot, and the friend was okay with that. At least at this point in time, Anne Marie was away from the drug addicts and drama.

Anne Marie had been working at the remodeling job a little over a week when her shoulder started hurting. She complained about it another two weeks until her friend told her, "Go see what's wrong with it, or shut up about it." Anne Marie thought that was good advice, so she went to the ER. Anne Marie thought she had simply pulled a muscle in her shoulder, and in time, it would heal. When the doctors asked her what she thought, she told them the story of moving a very heavy door and thinking she just pulled a muscle, then when she tried to get out of the bath tub she couldn't pull herself up.

The doctors ran a lot of test and finally told Anne Marie she had pneumonia in her left lung. They admitted her to the hospital right away. All Anne Marie wanted to do was smoke a cigarette because it had been a long wait to see a doctor. She called her daughter, Amelia, to come to the hospital and get her things. Anne Marie barely remembered doing that, but as soon as Amelia arrived, Anne Marie told her she was signing her power of attorney over to her and she had to make all the decisions. This was an awesome responsibility to give someone so young. The last thing Anne Marie remembered was setting on the side of the bed. Anne Marie found out later that it had all happened two and a half months before. She had been placed in a drug-induced coma. She nearly freaked out. She had no way of knowing how bad she had been. All she remembered was going to the hospital but for the past two and a half months of her life; she had no recollection of where she had been or what had happened. She asked Amelia what had happened, and she told her the following:

They had to put a tube in her lung for it to drain. When they did, her lung collapsed, and all her organs started shutting down. They then placed her in ICU and told Amelia and the rest of the family—they did not expect her to recover. They had put her in a drug-induced coma and inserted a ventilator so she could breathe. Amelia relayed to Anne Marie that the doctors and nurses knew she was a drug addict by the needle marks up and down her arms plus her blood test. They called the family more than once to say good-bye to Anne Marie because they thought she was dying. Momma, Rachel, and Cade were all pretty scared because Maddie had died just six months before in the same hospital. Rachel came every day to visit Anne Marie, and she would rub her legs and arms with lotion and talk to her. On more than one occasion, she had words with the nurses because she feared Anne Marie was not getting the care she needed because she was a drug addict, and most of them thought she was going to die anyway.

After two and a half months on the ventilator and in a drug-induced coma, they tried to get Amelia to pull the plug and let Anne Marie die. Amelia refused; she would not hear of it and tenaciously stood her ground. After they did finally take Anne Marie off the ventilator, they put her on antipsychotic drugs. The drugs made Anne Marie hallucinate. She would see things that weren't there and talk to dead people. At one point, she thought she had a baby and was rustling the covers looking for it. It was a terrible sight for Anne Marie's family. The hospital staff moved her from the second floor ICU to the fifth floor ICU, and Amelia instructed them to take Anne Marie off the antipsychotic drugs. Amelia reasoned that if her mother was going to die, Amelia wanted her to die in her right mind, not hyped up on some drug. The doctor complied, and Anne Marie started to wake up and know what was going on around her.

During one of the episodes, a chaplain came in to give Anne Marie last rites. The chaplain was a female named Grace Langston. When Grace visited the sober and awake Anne Marie, Anne Marie was not nice to her at all. In fact, she ran her out of the room and told her to never come back, but the determined chaplain kept visiting her, and soon Anne Marie realized she was a gift directly from God. Being stuck in a hospital bed and unable to walk or go anywhere gave Anne Marie time to think—something she wasn't used to. Normally, she just reacted and didn't think about what the consequences would be for her actions. Now, all she had was time to reflect on her life and decide what she was going to do with her future if she was blessed enough to have one.

One day, Dr. Shatzer came in and told Anne Marie he was going to have to do surgery on her lung. He said she had so much infection in the lung that the only way it would get better was if he went in and scraped the lining of the lung. The tube in the lung was siphoning out what looked like sand to Anne Marie. She consented for the operation in hopes that it would help the healing process. The doctor scraped her lung and peeled the lining from the outside of the lung, leaving Anne Marie in worse shape than she was before. The doctor left four holes in Anne Marie's left side that wouldn't heal. One day, he came in and said he was going to have to do surgery again, and Anne Marie informed him he was never touching her again. She called him a butcher and every other word that she could think of. Finally, one of Dr. Shatzer's associates came in to talk to Anne Marie.

The new doctor's name was Dr. Willet, and he had a calming demeanor about him that gave comfort to Anne Marie. He explained to her that damage had been done to the lung, and he had to try and rectify it. Anne Marie finally consented to let Dr. Willet operate again. He removed two and a half ribs and the top portion of Anne Marie's lung. Between the first and second surgery, Anne Marie got a staph infection that resulted in a month of isolation. Anne Marie now weighed 96 lbs. She looked like a skeleton lying in her bed. One day, she called the nurse to help her go to the bathroom only to find that her legs no longer would hold her up, and she fell and hit her head and had to be rushed down to the ER to have it sewed up. Anne Marie prayed God would just let her die.

Anne Marie's veins would blow because of the abuse they had endured over the years, and the medicine she was on was so strong they couldn't carry it for long. Finally, they put in a central line that could be used to collect blood and give medicine through. Anne Marie breathed a sigh of relief. It was nice not to be prodded and probed on a daily basis. But time was beginning to wear on Anne Marie in addition to the sickness she had. She became very depressed, and the nurses would move her to another room with a different view.

Anne Marie didn't have many visitors. Momma came every chance she got, but she had no car and lived a great distance from the hospital. Anne Marie talked to family and friends by phone, but she realized they all had lives to live, and she was the only one stuck in a hospital bed. Often Grace Langston came by and talked with Anne Marie. Somehow their talks always ended talking about God and his merciful grace. One day, Anne Marie asked her momma to bring her Bible to her. When she got the Bible, she realized she hadn't opened it in years, and she started thumbing through it. Between the pages, she found slips of paper with scripture written on them. Scriptures she had written down while she was in jail. Suddenly, a slip fell out, and she picked it up to read. Years before on November 22, 1998, when Anne Marie was going to church and serving God, someone gave her a prophecy that she had written down. At that time in her life, Anne Marie didn't have a clue as to what it meant. As she lay in her hospital bed years later, the meaning suddenly became clear to her. The prophesy was, "I shall not die, but live to tell of all his deeds The Lord has punished me, but not handed me over to death" (Psalms 118: 17–18, The Living Bible.). Tears started to roll down Anne Marie's cheeks as she realized God had saved her, and this had been told to her years before. Years before when she was trying to live for the Lord, and he had told her she would not die. She opened her Bible to Psalms 118 and reread verse 17. Then she read verse 18 and that really jerked her up. "The Lord has punished me, but not handed me over to death." Anne Marie's frail body shook with emotion. Clearly, the Lord had saved her as she lay so close to death. His mercy and everlasting love had shielded her. He had given her another chance to get right with him, another chance to see her children and grandchildren, another chance at life. Anne Marie reflected back over her life and how she had ignored all the things that were important and opted instead to follow her own selfish ways. She had ignored the free gifts of God, like walking barefoot in the sand and grass, hearing the birds sing their beautiful melody, hearing a child's laughter. She took it all for granted and never once thought how blessed she truly was. The realization that most of the things she was facing were things she had brought on herself. She called it bad luck, but in actuality, it was God who placed road blocks in her path, all of which she would jump over and keep traveling the path she chose instead of walking the path God had chosen for her.

On June 26, 1999, Anne Marie had been given another prophecy. "'Not by might, nor by power, but by My spirit says the Lord" (Zechariah 4:6). Anne Marie realized during all the things she had been through, all the things she had done, God had remained every faithful to her, protecting her, giving her second, third, and fourth chances to change her ways. And she had spit in his face. She had mocked his very being. Tears rolled down Anne Marie's checks and soon erupted into sobs of anguish and pleas for forgiveness. But all these things gave Anne Marie hope that she could once again have a relationship with her Heavenly Father. For the first time, Anne Marie admitted to herself that she was angry with God for taking her friend Greg away. That had always been Anne Marie's excuse for drinking and doing drugs. That, and her daddy Johnny's molestation. Alcohol and drugs were the things Anne Marie used to still the hurt and anger she felt inside. Her shock was that God had heard and understood the language of her tears. All these years, he had stood waiting for her to realize he never left her. It had taken a severe illness, a walk through the valley of death, her lying flat on her back with nowhere to look but up, for Anne Marie to realize none of this was

God's plan for her. Even when Maddie died, Anne Marie asked God why he took the good one and left the messed up junkie. Her rationale now told her Maddie was ready to meet God, and Anne Marie was not. It had been eight and a half months, 121 days since Anne Marie had walked into the ER that fateful night. She was going to get to go home. Her excitement was overwhelming as she waited for Rachel to pick her up from the hospital.

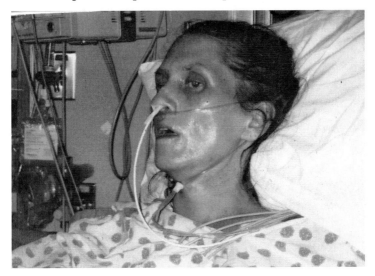

12

Even though she was home, Anne Marie was still very, very ill. A nurse would come by daily to change the dressing on her wounded body. The tube that had been in her lung was removed, leaving a huge hole that had to heal from the inside out. When she got home, the hole would make a noise when she breathed deeply or coughed or sneezed. Air was escaping her lung. The nurse cleaned the wound and packed it with gauze. One day, she told Anne Marie the wound was not healing properly, and she thought it was getting infected. She cleaned and looked at the hole in Anne Marie's side, and she said, "There's something inside of this wound." Taking a pair of tweezers, she gently removed the foreign object. To Anne Marie's and her amazement, it was an old piece of gauze that had been left in the wound for a very long time. The smell was overpowering, and it was evident why the wound wasn't healing properly. After that day, the wound started improving.

Anne Marie reflected back on the times the infectious disease doctor had stuck a Q-tip in the open wound to see if the staph infection was still there. Each time, she would shake her head and tell Anne Marie the wound was no better. On more than one occasion and from more than one doctor, she was told she might have to go to Galveston and have the lung removed. Each time, Anne Marie would shake her head and tell them, "No I'm not going to have to have it removed. Jesus is healing me." But the one thing Anne Marie seemed to be consistent about was her drinking. She got out of the hospital on December 4, 2003. By New Year's Day on 2004, she was back to drinking beer.

Before Anne Marie became ill, she had not reported to her parole officer in about two months. After that, she had been in ICU totally out of it. Her probation officer had not heard from her in over four months. As soon as Anne Marie could, she called Nell and told her what had been going on and why she hadn't reported. Nell had been a probation officer a long time, and she had lots of savvy about liars. She checked out Anne Marie's story. When she found that indeed Anne Marie had been in the hospital all this time, she understood and worked with Anne Marie. She told Anne Marie that she was getting ready to revoke her probation when she heard from her. She reminded Anne Marie that the state of Texas owned her. She was a four-time convicted felon on probation with eight more years to serve. After that, all Anne Marie had to do was call Nell and report how she was doing. Of course, Anne Marie always lied and said she was doing good when in actuality, she was back to smoking pot and drinking beer until she blacked out. She had gone into the hospital addicted to meth; she came out addicted to morphine.

Anne Marie despised the way the opiates made her feel, but she loved the way they stopped the pain. She was prescribed morphine patches, Lortab, and high dollar antibiotics. When she got in a lot of pain, she would put the patch on, but then she discovered if she took two Lortab and drank three tall boy beers, it would knock her out. She preferred that to the patches. So she sold the patches on the street and finally started selling the Lortabs too. Coming off the opiates was one of the hardest things Anne Marie had ever had to deal with. Her skin felt like crawling and trying to turn inside out. She hurt all over, and nothing made her feel better except more beer.

Anne Marie was out of time. She had to start going to probation and taking the classes the State of Texas said she was to take while on probation. She had to take Life Skill classes, drug offender classes, and do community service. She had to go to AA meetings and keep reporting monthly to her probation officer.

While Anne Marie had been in the hospital, social workers had applied for Social Security disability and SSI for her. When she was told financial help was coming, she was thrilled beyond words. The money finally arrived, and to Anne Marie's delight, she found she had a lot of back pay coming, enough to buy a car. At last, Anne Marie had wheels and money in her pocket. She was living large. She had to spend one week end in jail to pay for the tickets she had received when she was driving Rachel's old car with no insurance, and Anne Marie had no driver's license at the time. She really didn't mind jail this time. To her, it was better than being in the hospital. However, it made Anne Marie very angry when she found she had to wait six months after all the classes to get her driver's license again. But there was nothing she could do but play by their rules. Something Anne Marie had never been very good at. She usually played by her own rules and got in trouble.

One day, Anne Marie met a guy named Trey. Trey had been in jail with Roy and Outlaw. He told Anne Marie that Outlaw was bragging about giving Anne Marie a hot shot. Anne Marie was totally shocked. She had no idea that Outlaw had wanted to kill her. That certainly explained the holes in her jeans and the sickness she had felt. But she never knew he had wanted her dead. She rejoiced that she was not around those kind of people anymore. She decided she wanted to go to a NA meeting. It was at a halfway house for men. When she arrived much to her surprise, Johnny was there. Her stomach immediately started churning as she looked into his eyes. He told her he had been sober for a long time. Anne Marie didn't believe a word he said. After the meeting, and seeing Johnny, Anne Marie wanted to get high. She decided she wouldn't go back to any more NA meetings. She feared if she did and Johnny was there, she would start using again. So she went home and had a few beers and smoked a bowl instead.

At the NA meeting, she had met a guy named Cody. He suggested Anne Marie might like the AA meetings better. She thought she would give them a try. After all, she had to attend some kind of meeting. She felt as though she didn't need the AA meeting that her problem was with drugs not alcohol. How wrong she was. She discovered later that she was not only a drug addict, she was an alcoholic.

Cody was a good guy. He rode a Harley, and he sort of took Anne Marie under his wing. He would come by her house to be sure she had transportation to the meetings, and they would talk. Cody had been a heroin addict, but he had been clean and sober for seven years. He encouraged Anne Marie to get involved in the different activities that AA sponsored. To Anne Marie, it seemed he was the first person who was interested in what she had to say since she had been out of the hospital. Cody would take Anne Marie for rides on his Harley, and they would go out and eat. He even got Anne Marie to go to a biker's church with him. She hardly knew how to act around sober people. At first, she just wanted to get the meetings over so she could go home and get high and get drunk. But somehow it seemed Cody knew exactly what she had planned, and he would see she went somewhere else. Anne Marie finally realized she was indeed an alcoholic. She recalled that every time she had ever been in big time trouble, alcohol was involved. It had been a vicious circle of getting drunk, regretting it, then getting drunk again to forget how guilty she felt. She hated herself for being so weak. She hated that the alcohol would take her to places she didn't want to go and keep her there longer than she wanted to stay.

Anne Marie would say she loved her kids, and she had loved her husbands; but in reality, the only one she ever tried to please was herself. She felt hollow inside, with little hope for her future. It was then she decided she would get an AA sponsor and try to work the twelve-step program. Connie was her first sponsor in AA. Anne Marie liked her, and they shared some of the same experiences. It was Connie who thought she needed to experience an AA conference. She talked a very hesitant Anne Marie into going to a singles conference at Lake Murray in Oklahoma. It sounded like fun to Anne Marie, but she had her doubts.

On the day Anne Marie was to attend the AA Conference, Connie and her husband drove her to the destination. Anne Marie was nervous because she didn't know what to expect, and she knew no one there. At first she was assigned a room with a couple from Texoma. However,

Anne Marie didn't feel comfortable with them, then a guy offered to let her stay in the cabin with him and some more men. Well, even Anne Marie knew that wasn't a good idea. Once more, divine providence stepped in, and the association gave Anne Marie a scholarship. She got to stay in a beautiful cabin with seven other females. Anne Marie finally smiled and settled in to have a good time.

Sobriety was new to Anne Marie. She didn't know if she was going to be able to remain that way. Often she would wonder if she even wanted to try and stay sober. Reality was much harder to accept than the elusive world of drugs and alcohol. Satan, the liar, would tell her to have just a little drink that it would help take the edge off, but Anne Marie hung in and soon the days became weeks, and the weeks became months for sobriety. She was starting to feel good about herself.

Connie, her AA sponsor, started making suggestions to Anne Marie about taking better care of her appearance. She told her to stand up straight and put on her makeup and pay attention to her hair. Anne Marie would look in the mirror, and the image reflected back to her, looked just fine. She loved her tie-dyed T-shirts and her Jesus sandals. So she decided she needed and wanted another sponsor.

Her new sponsor's name was Sylvia. To Anne Marie's surprise, Sylvia was a registered nurse; and to make things even more ironic, she had taken care of Ann Marie in ICU those many months that sickness had kept Anne Marie in the hospital. She called Anne Marie the miracle child because she never thought Anne Marie would survive.

But God had other plans for Anne Marie, and this was becoming more and more apparent.

Growing up, Anne Marie thought she had to say yes to everything even if she really didn't want to. She thought sex was a tool you used to get what you ultimately wanted. It didn't mean anything to Anne Marie. She considered it a form of acceptance or attention from others. But AA was teaching her that sex was a beautiful thing to be shared by two people who loved each other.

Cody, Anne Marie's biker friend, didn't have to come by and take her to meetings anymore. Anne Marie now was comfortable going to the meetings alone. Anne Marie thought about Cody with thoughts of kindness because he had filled a void in her life when she so needed someone to help her. And even though they had slept together, they both agreed they were better friends than they were lovers. This had awakened the knowledge in her that she could have male friends without sleeping with them. It had made her realize how much she had accomplished and how good she felt about herself. One morning, years after their friendship had faded, Anne Marie heard that Cody had overdosed on heroin. Anne Marie sobbed with tears of anguish about her friend of long ago, who had cared and nourished her desire to get sober. She wondered in sadness, what caused Cody to start back using heroin. She knew he loved God and had helped so many obtain sobriety. With tears streaming down her face, she whispered, "Thanks, Cody, for your time with me. May you rest in peace." Anne Marie caressed Cody's memory and in so doing, realized life was so uncertain, and often, so unfair.

One night at a AA meeting, Anne Marie met a guy named Darren. He recognized Anne Marie and made a point to speak to her. He told her that one night, she and Sarah had stopped by his apartment and smoked a joint with him. Anne Marie had been drunk, and though she vaguely remembered the apartment, she didn't recognize him. As their conversation continued, Anne Marie remembered Sarah and Darren had been friends for a long time. During the course of the exchange, Darren casually asked Anne Marie if she would like to go to a Rangers baseball game.

Anne Marie had never been to a professional baseball game so she said yes.

When Darren came to pick Anne Marie up for the game, he had his daughter, Constance, with him. She was a freshman in high school, and Anne Marie thought she was as cute as a button. Darren took his daughter by her friend's house where she was to spend the night. Then they continued their journey to Darren's sister's house where they were to join them and go to the baseball game together. Anne Marie popped the Rangers sun visor hat Darren had bought for her on and thought, *That was nice of him to get this for me.*

The baseball stadium was beautiful, and for the first time in a very long time, Anne Marie relaxed and had a wonderful summer evening. It had been a very nice first date. After that night, Darren and Anne Marie started spending a lot of time together. Anne Marie told him up-front that her husband was in jail, and she didn't want to get serious about anyone else because if she could, she was going work things out with him. Darren didn't seem to mind. He just continued to call her, and on occasion, they would go out. One night, he invited her over for dinner and a movie.

Anne Marie smiled in the darkness as Darren put his arms around her and drew her close to him. For some reason, she felt safe and secure with Darren. She had not felt that way in a very long time. After that night together, Darren would come to Anne Marie's apartment to just spend time with her. Darren brought a lot of normal things back into Anne Marie's life. He pampered her and paid attention to her and made her feel beautiful. Although fourteen years separated Darren and Anne Marie in age, they had a lot in common, and she enjoyed just hanging out with him.

Anne Marie still would write Roy on a daily basis, and somehow she always manage to send him a $100.00 every month so he could go to the jail commissary. The last time Anne Marie had seen Roy was almost two years. Roy was in prison in far west Texas, and Anne Marie had no wheels. One of the girls in AA with her told her she would take her out there if she wanted her too. Anne Marie jumped at the offer, and soon she was traveling the road that was long and winding in the Western High Plains.

In wide-eyed wonderment, Anne Marie gazed at Roy across the table from her. The prisoners and their visitors were not allowed to hug, but they could hold hands. She thought, *He's changed so much. He doesn't even look like Roy anymore.* Out loud, she asked, "How are you holding up?"

He gave Anne Marie a familiar smile and said, "I'm fine. How have you been?"

Anne Marie could not get over Roy's appearance. He was covered in tattoos, and his head was shaved. He told her he now belonged to a white supremacy group. Anne Marie didn't know much about them, but she did know enough that she wanted no part of them. In Anne Marie's mind, she knew she and Roy had very little in common when they both were sober. Anne Marie prayed that if they were meant to be together, God would show a way; and if they weren't, he would place road blocks that would make their union impossible.

When Anne Marie got back from her visit with Roy, she called Rachel and asked if she would like to take a little trip to Oklahoma and just spend some sister time together. Rachel gladly accepted, and soon they were sitting on the shores of Lake Murray and talking together as they never had before. They shared their childhood secrets of the molestation at the hands of their daddy and how it made them feel. They talked about their mother and their siblings and then Rachel said, "I've got a confession to make to you, Anne Marie. That night you went to jail for not checking that boy's ID, Cliff and I slept together."

Anne Marie could hardly believe her ears. "You what?" she asked.

"I'm so sorry, Anne Marie. I don't know why it happened. The guilt I feel about it has followed me around like a dog. I'm so sorry," Rachel said with trembling voice.

"I can't believe that SOB has let me feel like I was the only one at fault in our marriage. He never once has uttered a word about ya'lls affair. Instead, he let me carry all the blame. That bastard!"

Anne Marie was furious. Not at Rachel but at Cliff for his hypocrisy. Rachel just kept apologizing, and Anne Marie just kept cussing Cliff.

Anne Marie rang the doorbell to Cliff's home, and he answered it. She started the sentence with, "You bastard, why have you let me think for all these years, that you were snow white with honor, and I was a fool for letting my family get away from me? Why didn't you at least have the courage and honor to tell me it wasn't all my fault?"

Cliff let Anne Marie rant, and it was apparent to her that he would have carried that guilt to his grave had Rachel not told Anne Marie about it. Finally, he said, "You don't have to carry the guilt by yourself anymore. I'm sorry."

Once Anne Marie's fury subsided, she realized her attack on Cliff was really not warranted. He had been a very good dad to their children and provided them a home when she was out running around and doing whatever she pleased. After all, at one time, she had worshiped the ground he walked on. She had spent sixteen and a half years of her life with Cliff, and together they had two beautiful children that she was so proud of. He would always have a place in her heart reserved just for him. God enabled Anne Marie to forget the past and look forward to the future.

The day that Anne Marie and Rachel had spent together was the beginning of relief for the both of them. The shared secrets, the talk about the room Anne Marie had inside of her that was crammed full of hurts and pains. So many that she had tried desperately never to go near that room unless she opened a crack in the door just long enough to throw something else in. The twisted thinking on Anne Marie's part that made her believe being drugged and drunk was the only way she could cope with life. Her many affairs and the many lies she told in order to just survive. Anne Marie put her hands over her eyes and sobbed with regret.

In the months that followed, Roy got out of prison. He came home to live with his mom. He and Anne Marie talked about getting back together, but it was as though Roy had recessed into a far away place that Anne Marie could not enter. He would allow Anne Marie to pick him up occasionally, and they would talk, but it was apparent to Anne Marie that their getting back together just wasn't going to happen. That was in the spring, and by July, Roy was back on drugs and going back to prison. One more time, Anne Marie realized God had protected her because had she been with Roy she would be going back to jail too.

Anne Marie contacted legal aid, and they helped her get a divorce. In one way, she felt very sad about Roy and her marriage being over. In another way, she felt relief because she realized their life together could never have been normal. Once more, Anne Marie put her past behind her and bravely turned to face her future.

13

When Anne Marie reached the fourth step in the twelve-step AA program, she shook her head and didn't know if she could accomplish what was being asked of her. The fourth step required that she take a moral inventory of herself. Anne Marie did not want to drag the past up that she had worked so hard to forget, but if she was to accomplish finishing step four, she had to work the program. Anne Marie confided in her sponsor Sylvia by telling her she didn't know if she could stay sober and work the step. Sylvia told her to work the step anyway. She had to face her demons, and the only way to do that was head on.

Soon after, Anne Marie started working step four. Johnny, her daddy, appeared one night at the AA meeting. The very sight of him brought such anger to Anne Marie that she trembled. He looked terrible. He was homeless, living on the street, and sick. For a brief moment, pity flooded Anne Marie. That quickly subsided when the thoughts of Johnny's abuse was remembered. At one of the meetings one night, Johnny asked her for money to buy cigarettes.

Anne Marie's first thought was to slap his face and tell him she had nothing for him. But instead, Anne Marie gave him money for cigarettes.

As the AA meetings went on one night, it was announced that Johnny had had a stroke and would the group please pray for him. That was a real hard thing for Anne Marie to do, but she did start praying for him. In the beginning, Anne Marie knew she didn't mean a word of that prayer. But as time passed, she did start to feel genuinely sorry for this man who had so scarred her life. Her counselor had told her she had to learn to forgive if she expected people to forgive her.

Anne Marie heard later that Johnny's wife had died, and that he was drifting on the streets. He had been living in a halfway house and got kicked out for drinking. Anne Marie tried one more time to help Johnny. Not because she had to but because she felt guilty about wishing him dead. It didn't take long for her to realize that she could not help Johnny, and all it did for her was bring back flashes of the past and cause her to want to drink or do drugs. The nightmares would start, and she would feel like a helpless child again caught up in the abuse over which she had no control. She went to Johnny and told him she forgave him, but she had to move on with her life. He nodded his head and said, "Thank you." That was the last time she saw Johnny alive.

Anne Marie started working on step four again. She was having a terrible time with this self-inventory thing. The next thing she knew, she was smoking a little pot just trying to relax. She called it a little marijuana maintenance. Sylvia, her AA sponsor, took her out of the women's Bible study group and put her back to work step one again. But hardheaded Anne Marie continued to smoke pot and ended up failing a UA test for her new probation officer, Mike Fuller. She had been doing very well, but then things seemed to just start falling apart. Mike asked her if she had ever been through rehab anywhere. Anne Marie told him no, but if he thought it would help her, she was willing to try. She had never had any kind of structured help, and Mike insisted she was a prime candidate for this type thing. He revoked Anne Marie's probation, and plans were made for her to be placed on a waiting list. The first bed that became available would be hers. One afternoon when Anne Marie arrived at her apartment, there was a note taped to the door that told her to call Mike Fuller ASAP. When Anne Marie made the call, Mike told her a bed was available, and she would be leaving soon. However, she had to spend a week in jail just to be sure she was clean when she arrived at the East Texas facility. She had taken some money with her to buy books and a few other things. The week she waited to go to East Texas was one of the longest weeks Anne Marie could remember. She was nervous and very anxious about what this new place would be like.

Soon Anne Marie arrived in East Texas at a large rehab center where she was committed for six months by the state of Texas. Anne Marie thought that this was much better than going back to jail, and the place was nothing like she had thought it would be. There were no bars and no fence. There was even a dog that lived on campus. The patients could wear their own street clothes and smoke cigarettes. It didn't take long for Anne Marie to feel comfortable. Then she found out her councilor was going to be a guy named Bob.

Bob had the reputation of being the toughest counselor on duty. He was a recovering alcoholic and an ex-marine.

Anne Marie felt uncomfortable about meeting Bob. Perhaps it was because she knew he couldn't be fooled. The fact that she was the oldest patient there didn't help either. She just generally felt out of place. Her first meeting with Bob went like this:

"Anne Marie Felts, Ms. Felts, are you aware you are the property of the state of Texas? You are here by court order. You will be here for a minimum of six months, longer if you do not cooperate. The state gives us permission to hold you up to two years. You, my dear lady, are a criminal. That is why you are here. You will get one phone call a week, and you are to stay away from the male population that resides on these primacies. Do you understand these rules?"

Anne Marie nodded affirmation, and thus her new life began in the rehab center. They didn't have to worry about her trying to hang around the guys because she was in love with Darren. He was all she could think about as she went about her daily routine. She was there for recovery, and recovery was what she intended to achieve.

There were seventy residents in the center and four counselors. The center had three phases a patient had to go through. Anne Marie was in phase one. They were all placed in groups, and Anne Marie drew the Musketeers group. Wouldn't you just know that was Bob's group? Anne Marie rolled her eyes when she saw her name in his group. *This should be interesting*, she thought.

Anne Marie found that being in a group and openly talking about some very personal things disturbed her. Communication had never been one of Anne Marie's strong points. But she attended the meetings, and she tried to keep an open mind.

She liked her room and roommates. She found them all to be pretty "cool." Two of the girls were even from the same county Anne Marie was from. They all were struggling from the rules and regulations that were set up for them so that gave them something in common from the beginning.

Darren, Anne Marie's new boyfriend, did not like the fact that she was going in for rehab. But Anne Marie assured him she was there for recovery, and that would help their relationship more than anything else she could do. Her work began, and she was a willing student.

Anne Marie made second phase the first time she tried. She was certain this would assure her she would be going home in six months. The fact there were people who had been there for much longer than six months, did not faze Anne Marie. She was determined she would do her time and in six months be released. She didn't think she would have to actually "change" to achieve this.

When Anne Marie made second phase, Bob told her she had to write her life story down. Anne Marie was not about to do that. That was too much like step four had been for her. She told him she refused. He told her all right she didn't have to, but she wouldn't get out of that facility until she did. Anne Marie decided if she wanted to get out, she better do what she was told. It took her over three months to get it on paper. Somehow, it seemed to Anne Marie, she felt better after having written her life story. It was as though a healing had started to take place.

In group sessions, Bob would ask her questions about things she had written. This angered Anne Marie because she didn't want everyone knowing her "business."

One day, Bob started in with questions to Anne Marie. He wouldn't let up. He kept on asking her and asking her. Anne Marie could feel the tears welling up in her eyes, and soon they were rolling down her cheeks, and she could taste their saltiness. She hated Bob for doing that to her. She came unwound like a cheap watch. She screamed and yelled and cussed him. She didn't care who heard her or what they thought. The tears and the rage were relentless. They continued for hours. Anne Marie had fought so hard to keep that door closed inside of her. She knew the anger and the monster that lived there. She didn't know what would happen or who would get hurt if they were brought out for all to see. But out they came with such a vehemence her roommates starred in disbelief. The door inside her was not just cracked a little; it was opened full wide. And Ann Marie's wrath rolled out like a giant Tsunami tidal wave destroying all that was in her path.

Anne Marie hated the fact that the door inside of her had been opened. She had kept it close and hidden from the world for so long that when she realized her counselor had blown it open she was furious. After her blow up in group session, she ran to the kitchen where she had been assigned to work. She started washing dishes, and the next thing she knew Bob was standing beside her. He told her to come to his office. Anne Marie could still feel her heart pounding in her chest when she entered Bob's office. Without being able to control her emotions, she knew she was going to be in trouble. She expected to be punished severely for her actions.

"Sit down, Anne Marie," Bob said. "You did good. I'm proud of you."

Anne Marie could hardly believe her ears. She had thrown the biggest fit anyone could ever throw and cussed Bob like a sailor. How could he be sitting there telling her she did good?

Bob continued on, "I want you to compile a victim's list. Put everyone on that list that you have ever hurt in any way."

With swollen tear-filled eyes, Anne Marie muttered, "That shouldn't take long. I'm the one who's a victim."

Bob just smiled and told her to do the list and then bring it to him. He excused her from work duty the rest of the day to go wash her face and calm down.

The coolness of her room felt good to her swollen eyes, and she picked up a piece of paper and sit down on the side of her bed. Reaching for a pen, she wrote the first name of a person she had hurt. When she finished, she was amazed at how many names there were on the list. She glanced at the clock and realized she had been working on the list for over an hour. Anne Marie was shocked she had hurt so many innocent people. Through her misdirection, so many people she loved had been directly affected by her actions. The tears started again as she thought that as a child she had been the victim, but as an adult, she had chosen to let others victimize her, and then she had become the victimizer. She had so cruelly left her children choosing drugs over them. She had grown calloused and hard, not caring how many others she hurt. She had pushed God out of her life. She was a criminal, and if she continued doing the things she was doing, she would continue to get the same results. *That truly is insanity*, Anne Marie thought, *repeatedly doing the same thing over and over expecting a different outcome.*

After that day of having the door inside of her opened, Anne Marie started feeling better about a lot of things. She had learned that she could control her fury and understand that all the really bad things that had happened to her since she had been an adult, she had chosen.

In order for Darren to get to come and visit her, Anne Marie had to do "I statements." These statements consisted of things that she was responsible for doing. The things she took full responsibility for. The things that no one else but her, had control over. She had to do these statements with Darren. That wasn't very hard because she and Darren hadn't been together through all of Anne Marie's alcohol and drug addiction, and if she wanted to go on furlough with Darren, these "I statements" had to be done. So together, Darren and Anne Marie worked through the assignment.

On one of Darren's visits to see Anne Marie, he quietly asked her to marry him when she got out of rehab. Anne Marie could hardly contain her excitement. She jumped in his arms, saying, "Yes, yes, yes." She was so happy. When Darren had to leave that day, Anne Marie looked after him as he slowly walked away. She thought her heart would burst at the thought of it being another month before she would see him again. The only thing that sustained her was her dreaming of the day she would be out of this place and be Darren's wife.

The six months Anne Marie was supposed to be in rehab turned in to seven, then eight, and longer. Some people came and went. People who had come in after Anne Marie were leaving, and she still was stuck at this place. One day, Anne Marie realized she was learning the lesson of tolerance, patience, and wisdom. Hard lessons to learn but lessons she knew she so desperately needed. The only thing that kept her going was the fact when she finally did get out of there, she would be with Darren as his wife. So instead of being mad all the time, Anne Marie decided she would smile and accept her fate. She had to only work on her recovery, and by doing that, she would make the time go faster.

One morning, Anne Marie realized she was feeling really bad. Normally, she would get up, go get a cup of coffee in mess hall, and her sleepiness would subside. But this morning, she was dragging, and the coffee didn't even help her. Her counselor gave her a 24-hour furlough to go to a doctor. To Anne Marie's surprise, they discovered she had been overdosed on her thyroid medicine. The center had switched the drug's brand name to generic, and Anne Marie couldn't tolerate the higher dose. Once the dosage was adjusted, she started to feel much better.

Time dragged for Anne Marie, but she found out that if she worked in the garden, it had a calming effect on her. So daily, she would go outside and tend the garden the residents had established. One day, she was pulling weeds when the thought came to her. *Weeds are like the sin in my life,* she thought. *It has to be pulled out roots and all, or it will come back. Some of the roots are deep and hard to uproot. Others spread like vines into other areas of my life. I have to get rid of the really deep rooted sins so that my life will have a chance to grow and be healthy.* Anne Marie grew excited because she realized, God had spoken to her heart in such a simple way that she could understand totally. She started looking forward to that quiet time alone in the garden, pulling weeds and knowing the Lord was right beside her. She was changing. At first, it was just in little things, and then her attitude about her life took on a new meaning.

Her son, Jacob, sent her an invitation to his graduation from high school. Anne Marie longed to attend that event. She could hardly believe that Jacob was so grown up. Where had time gone? She had missed most of Jacob's childhood. How could he ever forgive her for the stupid mistakes she had made? She had hurt him so badly. She knew he felt as though she had abandoned him, and in reality, she had to accept the fact that she had done exactly that. How could he ever forgive her? Anne Marie's heart broke as she recalled the mistakes made in her life. She had never sat out to hurt anyone, yet through her selfish behavior, she had left broken hearts behind her. Innocent hearts that she could never go back and undo the things she had caused. She silently prayed that somehow God would heal the hurts she had inflicted on the people she loved so much. Her prayer was that someday her children would be able to forgive her for her misguided life.

Darren came and got Anne Marie and saw to it that she got to see her son graduate. Anne Marie knew she didn't deserve to get to attend one of the most important events in Jacob's life, but she was so thankful she did. Darren's kindness to her and her children only made Anne Marie love him more. She realized Darren had driven for hours to make her dream come true. He had sacrificed his time and his money just for her.

Darren had taken care of Anne Marie while she was in rehab. He had seen that she always had money on her books to supply some of her needs. He came to see her every chance he got, often bringing her children with him. He spoiled Anne Marie in ways that no one had ever done before. Anne Marie could hardly wait to go home and marry Darren. She looked forward to growing old with him. Each passing day, her love grew for this man that she felt God had given her, and she quietly and privately whispered her gratitude in God's ear.

Anne Marie and Darren started talking about their wedding plans. Obviously, Anne Marie had no way of planning a wedding and making the arrangements, so

Darren did it all. He would have his sister help him, and then they would ask Anne Marie if she approved. Darren would mail pictures of dresses that he thought Anne Marie would like and let her pick what she wanted to wear to their wedding. It was going to be an outside wedding, Anne Marie insisted. She wanted to go barefoot, sort of hippy style. While they had been home for Jacob's graduation, Darren's sister had made their picture to post in the newspaper announcing their engagement. All they needed was a date. Finally, September 19, was the date the center told Anne Marie she would be released. It was one day shy of a year since she had first walked through the doors of the rehab center. Her life had changed in so many ways she could hardly believe it. The shackles of alcohol and drugs had been removed from Anne Marie, and she could breathe the sweet air of freedom. Freedom from her old self and her old way of life was precious to her. It was as though God had reached down and personally removed the chains that had held her captive.

On September 23, 2006, four days after Anne Marie got out of rehab, she became Darren's wife. Her dreams had finally come true. She was married to the love of her life, her husband, lover, and best friend. Anne Marie's life had changed so much that she hardly recognized the person she had become. But challenges lay ahead for Anne Marie that would test her faith in God and her newfound sobriety.

14

Anne Marie was so excited. Darren had announced they were going to start looking for a house to buy. She could hardly believe it. She was actually going to have a home of her very own. Darren had said so. He relayed to her that he needed to be closer to work. The amount of miles he was driving was killing him. He left home before daylight and arrived back after dark. He spent more time on the road and less time with his new wife, and he didn't like that, so they were going to start looking for a place to buy that's closer to his work.

Every weekend, they would go out to various towns around and close to where Darren worked. Every weekend, they would get back to their apartment totally worn out and not have found anything that appealed to them in the price range they could afford. One Saturday morning, they decided they would drive to a small town located about twenty six miles north of Darren's place of work.

When they arrived in the small town, Anne Marie looked around with curiosity. She had never lived in a small town before, and she didn't know if she really liked it or not; but she was determined if Darren found something he thought they could afford, she would be happy and would go along with his decision. They started driving up one street and down another. In a small town, it doesn't take long to see every house that calls that town home.

A small sign caught their attention, and they stopped to look further. A yellow and tan house with turquoise trim caught their eye. "Well, we can always paint the turquoise trim," Anne Marie blurted out.

"Well, it does have possibilities," Darren said.

They quickly got out of the car and walked to the back door. The back yard was big, and Anne Marie visualized all the wonderful things they could do out there. "What do you think so far?" Darren questioned.

"I think we can do most of the work ourselves and make this a pretty little place," Anne Marie said.

"I agree. Let's get the name of the realtor off the sign and see if we can get in."

When they called the realtor listed on the sign, she agreed to meet them at the house and let them look around. After greetings were exchanged, the realtor unlocked the door to the house.

The rooms were nice sized, and Darren even picked out the room he thought would make Anne Marie a really nice art and craft studio, and soon they were signing the papers on their new home.

Days, weeks, and months past, and Darren and Anne Marie spent every minute they could, painting and fixing up their home. Darren would work on the weekends, and Anne Marie would paint during the day when Darren was at work; and before long, the ugly turquoise paint had transformed into a beautiful shade of ivory, and their house started looking like their home. Anne Marie would reflect on her wonderful life now and whisper prayers of thanksgiving.

One day, Anne Marie decided she needed to go into a larger town and buy some groceries. She exited her car with a smile on her lips and a grocery list in her hand. She started down one of the aisles, and she heard someone calling her name. Turning, she saw one of her old friends from days past waving at her. She returned the wave and made headway to the friend. They hugged and exchanged greetings and in general got caught up on the years they hadn't seen each other.

"So what are you doing, Donna?" Anne Marie asked.

"Trying to stay clean and sober," Donna replied, "but I'm having a hard time doing that in my line of work."

Smiling, Anne Marie asked her, "Are you still ——?"

"Yeah, every chance I get. It's hard to raise kids these days by yourself. I've tried to get out time and again, but nothing makes me that kind of money," Donna said with a sorrowful look on her face.

Anne Marie remembered the days of drugs and alcohol, and a wave of pity swept over her for her longtime friend.

"Donna, why don't you go to a rehab center like I did and see if you can get help. As long as you're prostituting, you're never going to be able to quit the drugs and alcohol. Girlfriend, you're not getting any younger, and you need to stop this insanity." Anne Marie said with absolute pity and encouragement in her voice.

"That brings up something I've wanted to tell you for a long time but haven't seen you nor had the chance to talk to you."

"What's that?"

"While you were in rehab, Darren called me over one night. I swear, Anne Marie, I didn't know you two were together until I saw the picture of you and your good friend on the wall. Then it dawned on me who he was and who you were. Had I known before, I would never have gone over there. I'm so sorry, Anne Marie, can you ever forgive me?"

"Of course, forget it, Donna. We weren't married then. Of course, I forgive you." Anne Marie had to rush to leave the store before she burst into tears in front of everyone. She hugged Donna and made her departure.

That night when Darren came home from work, Anne Marie confronted him with her friend's accusations. Of course, he denied every aspect of the sexual part but did admit Donna had dropped by one night to ask him for money. She had stayed long enough to drink a beer and then left. Darren swore to Anne Marie that's all that happened. He had been true to her from the day he had asked her to marry him, he stated.

Anne Marie looked at him with anger. Not saying anything, she went in, took a shower, and went to bed. She had to think about this thing that had come up, and she knew she had to resolve it, or she could never stay married to Darren and remain sober. Her very soul had been shaken. She loved Darren so much. She had put him up on a pedestal. She would never have believed he could betray her, yet her friend's statements all seemed to be true. Anne Marie prayed hard that night for the Lord to send her the answers she needed.

When Anne Marie awoke the next day, the sun was streaming through the window of her home. She could hear the birds singing outside, and on the table, she found a note from Darren. It read,

Anne Marie, I love you with all my heart. I do not know why Donna would have told you I slept with her while you were in rehab, but it's not true. Please believe me."

Love, Darren

Anne Marie stood staring down at the note she held in her shaking hand. She looked out the window to her back yard that Darren had worked so hard to make beautiful. She thought of the hard work he did every day to make their living, and tears welled in Anne Marie's eyes.

She whispered, "Thank you, Lord, for giving me the answer. How can I not forgive Darren and give him benefit of the doubt? You have forgiven me so much. Am I to do any less for those I love?"

When Darren came home that night, Anne Marie greeted him at the door and said, "Will you forgive me for doubting you? I love you, Darren."

The subject of Donna and the night she came to Darren's apartment while Anne Marie was in rehab was never mentioned again by either Darren or Anne Marie. If it had happened, only Darren would know, and he would have to live with that. Anne Marie knew she had to forgive people if she expected to be forgiven, so she made up her mind she would forgive and go on with her life. In rehab, they had taught her, "You're only as sick as your secrets." She was determined she would not return to that dark place where secrets hide and hold you captive.

⚭

Anne Marie awoke with coughing she could not control. She got up and went to get some cough syrup. She downed it quickly, waiting for the coughing to subside. For a moment, it seemed the cough syrup was going to help, but then the coughing started again and racked Anne Marie's body. Suddenly, she looked down, and blood was dripping onto the Kleenex she held in her hand. With disbelief, she stared down as the red stain spread and left traces on the Kleenex.

What could this be? Anne Marie wondered. *What could be causing me to bleed from my lungs?*

With horror, she remembered the days she had spent in the hospital and the many surgeries she had endured on her lungs. Fear griped her as she reached for the phone to call Darren.

When they arrived at the emergency room, the doctors quickly took over. They ran an MRI and did blood tests and were finally able to get the bleeding stopped. Then they talked with Anne Marie and Darren. They told them they couldn't find exactly where the blood was coming from, and they thought Anne Marie needed to stay in the hospital and be seen by a pulmonologist. He would be better equipped to handle the lungs. Anne Marie agreed, and she waited patiently for the specialist to come in and see her.

When the pulmonologist came, he told Anne Marie she had to have a bronchoscopy, so he could look at the lung. She agreed, and they scheduled the procedure to be done the next day.

When the bronchoscopy was over and Anne Marie was back in her room, she leaned her head against her pillow and took a big sigh. *Now, what's wrong?* she wondered. She thought of the months she had spent in this very hospital when she was so sick. She thought of the times the doctors had told her daughter, and her family, they didn't think she would live through it. She thought of all those things, then she turned her eyes upward and prayed, "I commit myself to your keeping, Lord. If you are ready for me to come home to you, then I am ready for that as well. I leave it all in your mighty hands."

The doctor entered Anne Marie's room and took a seat next to her bed. "You have Aspergillosis," he said. "That's a fungal infection that we are not equipped here to treat. You are going to have to go to an infectious disease doctor for treatment."

Anne Marie's heart skipped a beat and then she said, "Is such a doctor available here?"

"No," the doctor replied, "We are going to refer you to a specialist at Baylor in Dallas. I'm releasing you today, and you can go home, but please call and schedule an appoint with this specialist as soon as you can."

Anne Marie nodded her head in agreement and took the specialist name and phone number when the doctor handed it to her. "Thank you, doctor, for your concern and care."

As the doctor left the room, he reinserted the fact that she must go see an infectious disease doctor immediately. Anne Marie just nodded in agreement.

Oh, Lord, she thought, *another round of doctors and hospitals. I just as soon go on to glory.* But that was not to be the case for Anne Marie.

The infectious disease doctor finished her preliminaries with Anne Marie and told her she had to be on antifungal medicines for a long while if they were to get the Aspergilla's under control. One of the medicines cost over $2,000 a month. Anne Marie knew that was never going to happen. She asked the pharmacy if there was a generic drug that was cheaper. They told her there was, and she phoned her doctor to see if she could take the generic instead of the more expensive drug. The doctor agreed, and Anne Marie was faithful to take her medication daily as instructed. Her improvement was only minor.

One day, one of the doctors told her she had three choices: continue taking the medicine that really wasn't that effective, another surgery, or an experimental procedure that wasn't proved. With this method, the medicine would be injected directly into the fungal ball that lurked in her lungs. Since nothing had worked so far, Anne Marie wanted to try the experimental way. The doctor told her it was risky as the medicine could cause kidney failure. She went home and talked it over with Darren. Then she decided she would just continue to take the antifungal medicines and trust the Lord to do the rest. For one year, she faithfully took the medicine and continued on with her life. At the end of that year, she felt better and thought that life was good. But should it end tomorrow, she was ready. She had tried to be the kind of woman God wanted her to be. She had overcome so many, many obstacles with his help. He had blessed her in so many ways that she could not even begin to count them all. She had seen her grandbabies born, strong and healthy. She had regained a personal relationship with her children. She had a loving family and a devoted husband. All these things she had been given, and she felt very thankful and so undeserving.

Often, Satan, the liar, would come to her in the still dark hours of early morning. He would whisper in her ear. He would try and tempt her to once again fall from God's grace and join him in the dark abbess that waited just outside the realm of Anne Marie's conscious mind. He would remind her of all the really wicked, depraved things she had done and then ask, "How can God really forgive you?"

Anne Marie would rebuke Satan and tell him to get behind her by the blood of Jesus. She would remind him that she was God's child, and neither he nor anyone else could take that away from her. As the Bible says, Satan has to flee at that command, but she knew he would be back with his temptations, and she would look toward heaven and utter the Psalm 23:4 over and over. Then, with a smile on her face, she would quietly repeat, "Yea, though I walk through the valley of the shadow of death, I will fear no evil: for Thou art with me."